Yassini Girls

First published in the UK by Beacon Books and Media Ltd
Earl Business Centre, Dowry Street, Oldham OL8 2PF, UK.

Copyright © Shereen Malherbe 2024

www.beaconbooks.net

Cataloging-in-Publication record for this book is available from the British
Library

ISBN 978-1-915025-94-4 Paperback
ISBN 978-1-915025-95-1 Ebook

Cover design by Raees Mahmood Khan

Yassini Girls

SHEREEN MALHERBE

BEACON BOOKS

Our writing is intended for us to own our stories because if we do not write our story, it becomes the property of our enemies.

Ibrahim Nasrullah

Layla.

EVERY FAMILY HAS SECRETS. Stories they don't tell you. I am no exception. There are people in my family who are no longer with us. What happened to them? No one knows for sure. I have only just been told at age thirty-five that everything I knew about my family history was not the truth. What I am about to discover will change everything.

I believed my family lived in Palestine, Ariyha (Jericho) on the farm where they had lived for generations. When I visited, I always stayed on the family farm. I will describe it to you as it was during my childhood because as I write now, the farmhouse is being demolished. Each piece of stone is being smashed to its very foundations. The glassless windows fall by its side. The memories inside it live on as it becomes dust in the ancient ground.

So as with anything that was, we must capture it in all its detail because it soon will no longer exist. In Palestine, this is happening rapidly. From week to week the landscape changes. It is stolen. It is destroyed from underneath people's feet. So here it is. A one-storey farmhouse made of stone. It has square windows with no glass inside them, just wrought iron bars over the windows and some mosquito netting with holes that could let a small bird fly through. The floor is stone and has been tiled in terracotta in places, and bare stone in others. The walls are bare. White-washed. There are three rooms, a bathroom, and a kitchen. The kitchen is a hob above a gas canister to cook the food, a sink and tap, and a pantry that my Tata always keeps filled with *baklava*. There are no cupboard doors; the pantry and the bottom cabinets are covered with floral cloth that hangs down and hides the utensils and saucepans underneath. On the stove, *maklouba* is cooking. *Maklouba* means 'upside down' and it is one of the oldest Palestinian dishes I know of. I researched it once. It was made for Saladin, the saviour of Jerusalem, to celebrate the capturing of the city in the twelfth century. It is served throughout Palestine and every family recipe is slightly different. In our family, we use cauliflower, and our spice mix comes from a spice shop in Al-Quds. This is the spice all of my family use. The chicken is boiled in a stock made of cardamom seeds, onion, black pepper, and some *maklouba* spice. Cauliflower is fried separately. The medium-plump rice grains are soaked. Once the chicken is cooked, fried off and the cauliflower is slightly brown and crispy, it is layered in the pan. Chicken first, then cauliflower, then the drained rice, and another sprinkling (half a teaspoon to be exact) of *maklouba* spice. Stock is added and it is simmered for twenty minutes.

During this time, we cut a salad of finely diced cucumber, tomatoes, lettuce, mint, and parsley. It is seasoned with lemon juice and salt. In my childhood, these ingredients were picked from our farm. Our family farm that we have lived in forever. Or so I thought. When the rice is cooked and soft, the pan is turned upside down (hence the name). If you are very good at this, the upside-down stays intact on the platter it is served on. It is a perfectly formed mound with chicken pressed into the surface and not a grain of rice falls down the sides until we begin to serve it up. We always eat ours with yoghurt. We eat under the grapevines laden with bunches of green grapes; the orchard wraps around the house, delicately scenting the air with the sweet smell of citrus fruits ripening under Jericho's sunshine, fed by the purest of springs that run through the ancient city.

The whole family gathers on the courtyard with us and pulls up chairs to eat. There are many of us there. I sit with my Tata. She has me on her knee whilst she scoops over and dishes up food. The threads on her *thobe* are close to me as she leans in. I trace them with my fingers, feeling each individually handmade stitch. Hundreds of them come together in elaborate, geometrically precise patterns. I trace them and the shapes they make. They tell a story of her life. One I wouldn't discover for decades from this moment.

If I walk down the street and take a wrong turn, I only have to mention the Zaghari family name and I am directed back to the farm. I sit looking out onto the street, facing the mountains in the distance. Temptation Mount is a famous site that was said to be where Jesus (peace be upon him) spent forty days and forty nights hiding from the devil. This place, both the mountain and the city, is a sanctuary. Underneath Temptation Mount are archaeological ruins that date Jericho as one of the oldest cities in the world. It is a UNESCO heritage site. With its positioning in the valley, its sunshine, and its springs, it has been a natural living place for humans since the start of time. The stories I have been told about the place come alive on its streets and in its traditions, in my own family's roots here. I feel an affinity with this place unlike any other. I spent the first half of my life writing about this idyll. The half of me that existed in Palestine is part of me. Yet, as the years pass, things begin to fall. Cracks begin to appear. Throughout the years, the toll of the Occupation worsens. The grip on Palestinian lives is tightening and suffocating them. The farm is dying. The water is being diverted to settlements; the farm is becoming a wasteland.

But this is not the secret. This happens in broad daylight under blue skies in a world that, mostly, looks the other way. No, what I am talking about is something that happened in my family that links me to its land forever in a way I couldn't have imagined. It happened as you would imagine it would happen in a story. Much like the novels I write. One day, I was told something that changed everything.

***

It is decades later. I am standing back in Jericho with a TV crew. I am not in the comfort of my family's courtyard and in the streets that know our name. This time I am in the desert outside of Jericho, surrounded by undulating dunes and an old mosque hidden by palms, tucked away on the side of the road. It is a beautiful old mosque that I have never seen before. There is a camel outside, dressed and waiting for tourists to ride for a few sheikal at a time. We are here early. There are no tourists around. The film crew pulls over up ahead. The taxi I am in pulls up behind them and the driver waits for instructions. We are waiting for trucks to pass by so they can film us driving through. They want to film me arriving in Jericho because they are going to tell me what happened to my family. I sit in the back of the taxi, looking at them set up the drone and filming equipment. The land that was so familiar to me now hides something from me and I am sick to the stomach waiting to find out what it is. I wonder what they are going to tell me. If it will change me. I have spent the last decade writing about Palestine yet here I am, like a stranger in its lands. It is hiding something from me. But it is part of me. I need to find out.

Fatima.

Chapter 1

THE KITCHEN IS A row of units along a wall and a gas hob, ignited by the gas cylinder underneath it. I cannot tell you how many times I have made *maklouba* on this stove, inside these stone walls. First, it was made for me by my mother and then I made it for my children and soon, I will make it again for my grandchildren and I will teach them. 'Limestone is formed by the precipitation of seawater formed over millions of years.' I remember, even though it feels as if a million lifetimes have passed, his voice. The composition of stone. It fascinated me, even as a child. How time has compressed the bones of the dead and turned them into stone.

I cut the cauliflower with a sharp knife. My fingers, despite my age, automatically dissect it for dinner. The phone rings. The distant ringing takes my thoughts away.

'Fatima, it is the film director again. He wants to talk to you.'

'You know today I am busy, *habibte*. I don't have time for this.'

'But he says he would like to ask you about Suad – a neighbour of yours –'

I drop the knife, and the clang on the stone floor drowns out the next words. All I hear is 'treasure'. I scoop down to pick up the knife, but I struggle to get back up. My body doesn't move freely. I lower myself to the floor and lay against the cold stone.

'Fatima, Fatima, are you okay?'

I close my eyes, pretending I can't hear. My brain unlocks and I see Suad. Not the Suads I have met since that bear no resemblance to her. I imagine my Suad. We are young again. She is vibrant and smiling. I hear her laugh. It sounds like an echo in the old stone. My Suad. After all these decades, she is now in front of me, leaning over me, whispering to me. 'Did you forget about us, Fatima? Did you forget about me?' She smells like almond trees in bloom. I imagine the blossom, fragrant in the air. The sun. Piercingly bright. I see another figure running out into the field. A figure of a young girl, a slight frame, a wisp of a dress lifted in the air.

I know why Suad is here now.

Suhair has moved me to my chair. Lovely, kind Suhair. She is my neighbour's daughter but sometimes I feel like she lives with me. I know she doesn't like me to be alone in the house, so she busies herself here. I don't mind. In fact, I prefer it. I like to hear the noise inside the walls, of life and footsteps, and of her happy humming as she prepares food or works on her *tatreez*. I was like her once.

She leaves me and tends to the dinner now the oil is unattended and spitting from the pan. I can't find the words to speak. I see the phone receiver hanging off the wall. Its tone sounds like an alarm clock, beeping. My time is running out. I reach out and touch the stone walls that my house is made of. I had a home once, a long time ago. It still feels strange, even after seventy-five years, to call this my house. It has been a faithful home. Its ancient stone walls have kept me safe, but I know more than most that stone does not protect something as fragile as life, as flesh and bones and blood.

I walk over to the phone and lift the receiver to my ear. He has gone. But he will call back. I know he will because what he asks about is true. Over the last seventy years, I have had many requests to talk about that day, but I have refused every single one. I do not like to remember it. I have spent an entire lifetime forgetting it. It is something I have wanted to forget, and I have become quite good at it. But then when I walk down the street, I hear it. '*Salam*, bint Yassini.' They know I was a Yassini girl and so it hasn't left me. I will always be a daughter of Deir Yassin. And today, I remember because I hear of her in that place. I hear of my dear Suad.

As the days pass after the phone call, something shifts. I no longer seem to live in the present. My mind slips back to seventy-five years, even longer, over eighty years ago. I am a child running through the gardens outside of the house my father built with stone. We are in the fields. I can see Jerusalem in the near distance. I am not alone either. They are all with me again. I can see their faces clearly as if they are standing in front of me. I can see them clearer than I can see my own grandchildren's faces. I think it is them. I think it is my siblings. We are all young, we are all my grandchildren's ages, and we are laughing and playing together. I sit and smile, imagining it. I close my eyes and I can smell the air of Deir Yassin. It is a scent of fig and almond blossom, and my feet are chalky white from the dust at the limestone cutting plant. It is carried in the air and settles like powdered snow around the houses. I see the black grapes my mother grows. I see my sister. She is a few years older than me, but she won't look at me and play with me like my brothers. My heart winces in pain as I recall her face. My eyes are closed but I am pleading with her to turn and look at me, but she refuses. I don't want to open my eyes until I see her. The old aches and pains have returned. Not from my ailing body but from the scars that are reopening under my memories. They are bleeding. Why did I do it? I was just a child, I tell myself, rocking my body to try and soothe the burden running through it. I was just a child too. I couldn't have known what was coming. None of us could.

I open my eyes with a start. My body is wet from sweat and Suhair rushes over. I notice the look of panic on her face. 'Don't worry, *habibte*, I am fine. Let's serve the *maklouba*. Everyone is due to arrive, and they will be hungry,' I say. I have many years of being a mother.

I will not eat because of the turmoil inside me. This could be my chance. My last earthly chance to make amends. I must take it.

I am in the house alone briefly as I have asked Suhair to go to the *souk* to collect some herbs for the salad. It is the time I need to speak to him, so I slowly punch the numbers into the phone and wait for him to answer. I ask of a name. He says he has found someone close. The film director is searching for it too. I can tell. After the pleasantries from the translator finish, he pauses, and I know what he wants to ask. 'There is a rumour of buried treasure, and I am told you know where it is. Is that true?'

Their hunt for treasure makes a small fire burn in the pit of my stomach. We had treasure once. In rolling fields and endless fruit trees, in golden sunshine, in a hilltop village overlooking the city. We had treasure once when we were a happy family, living together with the wonders of childhood and life dancing in front of our youthful eyes. In the wealth my baba built with his own two hands, carving the million-year-old stone out of the earth. In an abundance of food. In a heart innocent of pain. But I don't say any of this. I know what they mean by treasure, but they search for such futile things that I will never tell them the whole truth. They violently extract anything they think of value. They are ripped from the earth, sold, and put in glass cages so others can look at them as they tell their own stories about these wonders they discovered. I know what they would do if they found it. I think of the mummies found in Qadisha Valley. Those infants now exposed, their carefully embroidered clothes stripped off their bodies and on display in museums. Infant girls found dead. Their mothers lay beside them. 'Why would anyone kill their own infant daughters?' they ask in horror. I know the answer to that. I have seen it with my own eyes. Listen to the story it is telling us, in the stitches in our clothes, in those that survive and in the history beneath our feet, above our heads, carved into this ancient city that is being built of my father's stone. Then you ask me to trust you with a treasure I have guarded my entire life? You ask too much. You take too much.

But I am using this as my opportunity. Well, why wouldn't I? I am one of the last survivors. I know they cannot ask anyone else. Just as they want from me, I want from them. He is my only chance. I agree to take part in the filming. Once I hang

10

up, I take a deep breath. I am about to open up a part of me I have long kept buried. Why now? For her. It is for her and the peace of my soul. And I do feel differently now. I feel like I have had many lifetimes. The 1940s were a lifetime ago, and each decade that has passed since then. I can separate it, and why now? Because my memory becomes a short loop. My days are shortening. They consist of prayers, sustenance, and sleep. I am slipping away from this world. The more I fall from this one, the more I am immersed in one I was part of a long time ago.

Layla.

Chapter 1

I SMELL THE SPICED cauliflower and I watch as the smoke drifts out of the Edwardian window, filling the air with its foreignness. It is a smell that reminds me of our Friday dinners together inside the steamed glass windows of the hundred-year-old house that I have inherited now.

I remember the same smells drifting through the window during my childhood here. Isn't it funny that we run from our childhoods only to find ourselves replicating them decades later? My children are here today because I miss being away from them. I had to see them even though it has only been a week since I left them to come here. I didn't want to come. Who wants to be anywhere that holds the ghosts of their past?

I watch Yousef and Hannah inside this home. It is a skeleton of the home it was during my childhood. The furniture is rickety and old; cheap furniture that wasn't meant to last a lifetime. It was only supposed to last long enough for him to find a way back home. The old Edwardian windows are covered with heavy curtains and even when they are pulled open, they still cover most of the daylight trying to shine through.

He died in that chair.

I look at the curve of its broken back and I remember him sitting in it. If I had known it was our last time together, I would have done things differently. I would have come more often. I would have stayed with him to stretch out every second. I would have asked him all the questions that now lay unanswered in my brain and repeat themselves on a loop. I look at my children. They give me life. They are young and innocent and they are untouched by half a lifetime of regrets.

I glance out to the conservatory. The sticks of the dead orange trees are withered and black. I told him they wouldn't grow here when I was just a child, standing there in the freezing winter as snow gathered on the roofs. I knew then, they would die. They are not meant for here. He was not meant for here. I remember his hands, soft like butter. Darker than mine. He has a scar down his left wrist. Shrapnel from his childhood, he said. He didn't say anymore. He never spoke of his past.

I am remembering the last time. Yousef was here with him. Dad was in the glass room, tending to his plants. Yousef ran in and jumped on his knee, bored of watching his sister's babyish cartoon programmes. I call him little Yousef. He is almost nine, but I don't think any of my children will ever grow up in my eyes. I will always see them as my babies. Yousef, learning to read with a slight lisp on his tongue, an adorable innocence and an absolute love for his grandfather; a connection I had never seen before, as if he belonged to him sometimes, not me. The two of them spoke, immersed in their own world that he created through his words, inside the glass room. In the summer it used to be warm in there, like the Jericho winters. He was showing Yousef the soil, how to plant the seeds, and how to support them as they grew. He was pointing to the sky, the position of the sun. He was teaching him. When Yousef left, my dad's face returned to its sadness as he glanced outside up to the sky towards the weak rays breaking through the clouds. I had no idea at the time that I would be trying to remember each word we said to each other. My memory replays it as I look through the glass into the empty room.

'What is it, Dad, what's wrong?' I had said.

He didn't answer.

I said it again, placing my hand on his. His hands are shades darker than mine. They didn't look like they belonged here under the pale sunshine. They belonged to a land that felt far removed from where we were. He interrupted my thoughts and pulled his hand away. 'I need to go home.'

'You are home, Dad.'

'No, not this house. Ariyha.'

The words ran smoothly off his tongue. Ariyha. His childhood home.

'That is a long trip from here, Dad. I am not sure it's a good idea.'

'I need to go. I need to go back before it's too late.'

'I don't understand.'

'Layla.' He held my hands and faced me, his eyes pleading with mine. 'There is something I must do. Something I promised my mother when she was alive.'

'Tata?'

He nodded his head. 'I have already waited too long. If it is too late, if I don't make it, I – I –'

'Okay, Dad, okay,' I said, trying to calm him down. He sat down, his body trembling next to his dead plants.

'It is buried up there,' he said, pointing above his head.

'What is, Dad?'

'The little I have left. It is buried. You must help me. For my mother, may Allah bless her soul.'

'What did Tata want you to do?'

'To go back. We need to go back. You need to go home. Will you come with me? Can I take you?'

'To Ariyha?'

He nodded his head and gripped my hands. 'Not just Ariyha. Palestine. We have family all over Palestine. You need to know and so do your children.'

'But I have been before. You took me as a child to the family home, to Tata's house. I know all about it, Dad.'

'But you don't know how it used to be.'

'I remember the stories you told me.' I sat next to him, his breath slowing down. What I'm saying seems to be helping him, so I don't stop talking. 'When I was a child. I remember, Dad. I haven't forgotten. I remember Tata's gardens. I remember the orchard of lemon and orange trees, the smell of jasmine at night-time, and how we sat under the grapevines. Remember, Dad?'

He nodded, but his eyes had wandered elsewhere, and I wanted to check in, check that he was still with me. I felt I was losing him.

'It wrapped around the house. Tata would find me playing there just before dinner. And every time I was underneath the trees, she would lift me into them. My hands gripped tightly and pulled out an orange. We sat in the shade. I ran my fingers down the *tatreez* on her dress...'

He stopped me at that point.

'Yes, her *thobe*.'

'Yes, I remember it all, Dad. I will tell Yousef and Hannah. They will know it as well as I do.'

'Layla, I haven't ever told you this.'

'You can tell me now, Dad. I am not a child anymore.'

He hesitated. 'There is another side to Palestine.'

'I know, Dad. I have spent my adult life writing about it.'

We sat silently. Both of our minds played out what the other knew.

One that I had read before. It had stayed with me; a dark stain on my childhood idyll. The orphans. On a cold evening over seventy years ago, a young woman called Hind Al-Husseini was walking through the Old City, Jerusalem, past the church of the Holy Sepulchre and saw fifty-five children huddled near the walls there. They told her they had no home to go back to. She placed them in two rooms to keep them off the streets but, increasingly concerned for their safety, she moved them into her grandfather's mansion. I read that she said, 'I swear to God that I will live with them or die with them.' She was thirty-one years old when she found the orphans abandoned after their parents were killed. She was the same age I was when I read it, so it was easy for me to put myself in her position. I imagined I was walking with her through those streets, looking at those children, and I wondered if I would have been as brave as her. The story has haunted and inspired me ever since.

I wondered what memories were passing through his eyes because they were frozen, staring into his past, and he didn't tell me what they saw. His fear scared me. He said, 'Come with me. I must go home. We can go together. For Tata and for you. I have kept something from you.'

I could tell from how he spoke that he wasn't thinking clearly. He was elderly and his health was deteriorating. He was too old to take such an arduous journey. That is what I told myself, anyway. I told myself I would not go back home with him for practical reasons, but part of me was also terrified of the unspoken between us.

He looked at me intently as though I knew what he was talking about. Then it came to me. At first, slowly. There was something when I was younger. There was something I had seen. The feeling came flooding back as though more than two decades hadn't passed. I had completely forgotten about that day. It had faded into the background of my life, but in that moment its relevance and its importance to me as a child resurfaced like a blow.

I had found something he wanted to keep secret. A photograph. I looked at his face. I wanted to find the words, to speak to him, to ask him what he was hiding from me. But I didn't get the answer I wanted as a child, and I knew I wouldn't get it now. He never spoke of his past and nobody was ever allowed to ask about it. That had always been a rule between us. A line that was never crossed. As though his life started when he had me.

I felt as furious and helpless as I did as a child. I was relieved when Yousef came in and broke the awkward silence. Even seeing my own son did not make me feel like more of an adult. Some things were just meant to stay buried, and I didn't have the strength to start digging.

We ate dinner quietly. Shortly afterward, we left. As we walked out of the door, he whispered to me, 'We will go there as soon as we can. Soon, you will know.'

I kissed him on the forehead and left. He was smiling. Happy. I remember being so confused at the time. How was he happy about it? Did he not realise how I felt?

I never did find out as we never saw each other again. I am ashamed that I was unreasonable. Did I tell him I loved him? I replay our last words in my head. Did I tell him?

I add the chicken, rice, and stock to the cauliflower pieces sitting at the bottom of the saucepan. I place the lid on as it simmers away. I go and sit in the glass room as the dinner cooks. The alarm from the oven beeps and makes me get up from where we last sat together. I miss him too. The feeling makes a bubble swell in my heart, and it rises to my throat. I wipe my eyes quickly and turn the saucepan upside down. We sit and eat.

'It looks empty almost. You work fast. How are you feeling?' my husband asks, but I am watching Yousef. He is looking at my dad's empty chair. His hand is extended out towards it, and his palm is open, as though he is waiting for him to hold his hand. He always sat at the head of the table and Yousef always sat next to him. I know he is thinking about his Sidu. Hannah is sitting next to him. She is younger; she doesn't realise anything is different yet. I realise I don't want them to stay here in this dark house that smells of their Sidu who is no longer here. It is too much for them. They shouldn't have come. I will clear up after dinner and my husband will take them home. I imagine our home together and I long to be back there. I want to finish this. It doesn't feel fast enough for me.

My husband asks me again. I answer him with logic as I am not ready for emotion. If I start, it will spill out of me, and I won't know how to stop it.

'I have almost cleared out the lounge as you can see,' I say, pointing to the labelled, organised boxes stacked around us. 'The decent pieces of furniture will be collected by the charity shop at the end of the week. It is just upstairs now.' I reach for salad and yoghurt and serve the children, feigning busyness so I don't have to look at him.

'How are you finding it?'

'The house was as I thought it would be. But I have the attic next. I feel like I shouldn't be in there. You know how private he is.' I correct myself. 'Was.''

I think to myself, private or secretive? I know which one I believe.

'It's a shame you didn't manage to make the trip with him.'

I drop my fork and it makes a loud clanging sound against the plate. I don't know why he would say that. 'There isn't much I can do about it now!' I snap, the guilt resurfacing in my voice. 'How could I have taken him anywhere at his age and in his condition?'

My husband takes a deep breath. I know he doesn't know how to answer that, so he changes the subject. 'I didn't even know there was an attic in this house.'

I stop talking this time. I remember how I found out. I was about eight when it had been left open one day and, in my excitement, I climbed the ladder, eager to see the place he kept so fervently under lock and key. He had slipped up that morning. He had been up there, and I could hear his footsteps on the ceiling and the rustling of papers and scraping as things were dragged across the floor. But he had gone out and forgotten he had left his secret den open, half suspended between the ladder and the landing. I jumped up and pulled it down, climbing into the attic.

Despite his frequent visits (the attic was his home office), it was gloomily lit. Under a desk lamp on the floor was a pile of paperwork. I tiptoed over as though he would be able to hear my footsteps. I brushed my fingers over the pile of papers. A folder slipped off the top and fell to the floor, scattering photographs onto the bare wooden floorboards. Faces stared up at me from places and people I didn't recognise. I knelt next to them and tried to push them back into the folder. Then, amidst them all, another face. It was like looking in a mirror. It was a photograph of me. I lifted it out and bent it towards the light. It was me. But the photograph was black and white. The scene in the background, I didn't recognise the place. It must have been decades old. How was this even possible?

'Layla, what are you doing up here?' my dad's voice boomed behind me.

I jumped and dropped the photograph behind my back.

'You left – I, erm – I wanted to have a look –' my voice stammered under his glare.

'Get out. This isn't for you. If I wanted you to know, I would have told you myself.'

I burst out crying and left it behind.

He found me in my bedroom.

'I didn't mean to upset you. In fact, it is quite the opposite.'

'I saw something –'

'You shouldn't have been there.'

'The photograph – the girl –'

'Forget about it, Layla. You are a child. Be a child. Leave

the past to me. Remember Palestine as you felt when I last took you and we went to the farm and –'

His voice drifts off. I am not thinking about our last trip there. I am thinking about the present. Was I the past? Was there another girl? A long-lost sister of mine I never knew of?

'Close your eyes and let me remind you.'

I closed my eyes, my head spinning with darkness. Then I listened to his voice. My mind imagined the story and I pretended to sleep. But something had altered. The image I had known was starting to crumble. The new images interrupted the Palestine I had built with him in my mind. I knew from his stories, from the way his voice shook that even he knew it now.

It was all too strange, but I didn't want him to feel sad. The sadness pervaded his life. When he thought I was sleeping, I could hear him crying. I wondered what his nightmares were made of, which ghosts haunted his dreams, where they could make a grown man cry in his sleep. Whatever it was, whoever she was, or they were, it scared me enough to not ask again. I didn't want to know who the ghosts lying between the floorboards of our house were. I hadn't even told my husband. And yet above us and now between us was a secret that I was afraid would tear us apart and change everything I thought I knew.

I cannot eat. All I can do is watch as my children do.

Fatima.

Chapter 2

IT IS FUNNY WHAT you remember of your childhood, isn't it? Your early years seem to be made up of a few short memories that play on repeat. My memories of it are bliss. I will tell them to you.

We had a beautiful stone house made by my father's two hands and mined from his stonecutting yard. We lived off the land, but money had come into Palestine over my lifetime through ways I never saw as a child. Money from the British. Their control of farming and produce had left many farmers poorer and obliged to work in construction and other industries that suited the British colonisation during the Second World War. But we weren't as affected. When farming had become less productive, my father had already discovered the value of the stone in a quarry in our village. The stone became renowned for its quality and cut, and it was because of the British and their mandate that all of Jerusalem be constructed with this stone that it became so lucrative. But it wasn't that for me. It was my dad's ingenuity. He had already begun to build a life for us with his two hands. The stonecutting yard was not easy work. He came back the colour of a mummy, covered in its white dust, but he was building the city, he told us. There were many nights he spoke of rebuilding the walls of the ancient city. His craftsmanship was legendary. He could effortlessly select the right pieces of stone. Each individual stone slab was carved by hand, yet they would be identical in size and shape. They would use them to rebuild the crumbling parts of Jerusalem. And as the money grew, so did our wealth and our family. The villagers built houses that climbed to the hilltop and we had beautiful views surrounding our home, where the spring air smelt of almond tree blossom and fresh dinners were cooked every evening after the call to prayer. Schools were being built to provide an education to the village children, so we didn't even have to leave to go to the neighbouring villages to attend school. There was hope that came with expansion, and ease.

I dreamt that I would build things just like him. Before Baba rebuilt the town, I would explore its underbelly with him and together, we would extract from it the secrets of past generations. It was, after all, the most inhabited city in the world and one of the oldest. I imagined then that I could protect its future.

My mother exuded a contentment I only dreamt of. She was a natural mother in every sense. I had a sister – Lulu, we called her. Two brothers who were born first, Mohammad and Ibrahim. Twins. A blessing to have birthed and survived twins, my mother said, ruffling the hair on their ten-year-old heads. She doted on us and so did our baba.

We would wake up with the sun and tend to our plentiful crops. My favourites were the almond trees and the fig trees that lined the village. As young girls of maybe four and five, we would run in the gardens and sometimes find ourselves on the edge of the cutting plants as the dust and noise flew into the air. The stonemasons hammering and smashing the huge pieces of stone. The dust billowed into the air and covered them in a fine dusting of white, so they looked like part of the stone. 'These stones are millions of years older than you and me. They were formed well before us, and if we do our jobs properly, they will be here long after we are dust.'

Standing there as a child, I was amazed by the process. I couldn't fully understand the concept of time. It felt like a wisp in the wind, a day from sunrise to dusk. The longest time I had ever passed was waiting for my father to come home after a day at work. Those hours stretched before me, and he was all I waited for. I felt like it was the same for mother too. She busied herself in the day, making our home and tending to us all. A cut knee, a thorn from the shrubs, a never-ending appetite, playtime, and stitching tiny *thobe*s for our dolls that had been bought in Jerusalem. But when he came home with my brothers and the family was together, dinner was served as dusk fell on our village and it was the centre of my world. There was nothing in it I ever wanted except this and my heart was full. I know that now, but I didn't know how blessed we were to have that then. If I did, despite being young, I would have savoured it more. I would have told them how they made me feel every single day. I would have told my brothers I was proud of how they were growing up. I would have been kinder to my sister. I would have helped my mother each and every single time she asked me. But we didn't know what was coming. How could we? In my darkest nightmares, I couldn't have predicted how my life would change. And I was too young to know what happiness was. I thought how we lived was just life. And I was too young to know how much I loved them. They were just constant. There. Home.

Sometimes when I wake up fresh from sleep, I see it as though time has stood still. I am a girl. The gentle breeze lifts my hair. The air smells of figs. The stone is warm from the sun. I hear my sister laughing. I hear my mother in the kitchen. I am back there that day. She is smiling whilst she is making *maklouba* in her kitchen waiting for my father to come back from Friday prayers. They will be slightly later today. There is a funeral they are staying for. I want to be back there with them all as though it never happened. I want to beg my father not to leave that morning. I want to believe that something that morning was off. Something in the air, in the way the birds sang, in the way the earth moved below my feet, that there was a warning of what horror was about to befall. But there was nothing except for the warm spring sun, the smell of ripening fruits, the innocent play of children.

I hear them now outside of my window. I hear the voices of children playing. Their voices reverberate off the stone alleyways throughout the *souk* outside my window and echo through into my living room. It makes it come alive. I want to get closer to life. I lift myself up out of my old chair that has curved to fit the shape of my body. I look at the empty one next to me. I use my stick and very slowly step down the stone steps and out into the *souk*. The children are playing and buying falafel from the stall. I wander slowly around the streets just outside. I don't go very far. Even before walking was this difficult, I didn't go very far. Deir Yassin is just outside of the city. Sometimes I think if I look up, I will see the houses and almond trees on top of the hills. I have never been back. They used to ask me sometimes if I wanted to, if it would help in some way, but I have never wanted to.

I am interrupted by a group of children darting in front of me; there is a crowd of them but as they disappear around the corner, I see a familiar figure. A young girl but with hair the same colour, the colour of dark honey. It falls to her waist over a dress I have seen before. She doesn't turn around. Lulu? It is as though my sister is here, so I call her name out loud. 'Lulu? Is that you?'

I am disorientated. Of course it isn't her. What a fool I look.

I have wandered again. This time I am down a side street outside an old stone mansion. They brought them here, you see.

Layla.

Chapter 2

ICLIMB THE LADDER. I am back in the dusty attic, separated by decades. But the feeling is the same as it was all those years ago. My heart thumps. I walk out onto the floorboards and switch on the lights. The paperwork is piled in stacks on his desk. A reading light highlights some papers and files with blank title pages. I push them aside. I know what I am looking for. I want the photos again.

I find many photos but not the ones I am looking for. Instead, I see him as a child standing in the orchard. The space around me fills with trees and dark green leaves, and bunches of citrus fruits hang in abundance. I can almost smell the zingy scent of citrus. The floor morphs into soft grass between my bare toes. I can hear the sound of birds in the distance and feel the warmth of the sun on my back. I am back at the farmhouse. I hear my Tata's voice calling me. It is as clear as the day that has bloomed inside the walls of the old house. She is calling me to her. I feel guilty for not going. I open my eyes and realise I miss her. I never saw her again after that trip. And now my dad has also left. I am alone. The darkness creeps back into the attic and the trees shrivel away in the recesses of my mind. I never made it to her, I realise. I never made it for Dad, either. I swallow, but a hard lump forms in my throat, and I find it hard to breathe. My body is riddled with selfishness.

I open the drawers of the desk. A stack of plane tickets is bound together with elastic. They are tickets to Amman, Jordan. If Dad were to go home, he would have travelled through the land border in Amman to reach Palestine. He went via Tel Aviv once, but he was sent back after five hours of being questioned. Arriving via Tel Aviv airport means Palestinians who enter that way will have access through the centre of Israel, so they don't like to accept them into the country via that route. So, Dad, like thousands of other Palestinians, would travel through Jordan. A trip to Jordan meant he was planning on going home. Every few years he had booked one, but the tickets since his mum had died had been left unused. I reread the last tickets in the file. They are not just for him. He had booked a flight for me. I check the date. I sit back, reading my name next to his. He had booked us a ticket. He was sure I would go with him. I didn't. I hold the ticket to my chest and cry.

I leave it behind on the desk and leave the attic, then I leave the house and get into my car. I don't realise how late it is until the neon lights from the car's clock show me it is approaching midnight. I am miles from home. I pull over into a side lane and wait there, wondering what to do. I know if I keep running, this feeling that has invaded my heart will never leave. I can distract myself for a while at home, with the children and the busyness of life, but every time something reminds me, I will be back here. Back here in the dark, with my own thoughts turning in my head. My dad had a dying wish. I have no choice but to turn back and discover whatever it was that was so important to him that he held on to it, buried away in secret, for a lifetime.

I return and wait until morning comes. When it arrives, I awake from my childhood bed. I go through the photographs and memories that I know of; the ones that created the Palestine I had always known and loved. I fill a storage box. I want to keep them at my house now and show the children when they grow up.

I clear the rest of my dad's books and old clothes into a pile for donation. There isn't much else left to do. The paperwork and disintegrated items that are no longer distinguishable go in the rubbish. I keep the last plane ticket in my pocket and throw the rest away. They were all to Jordan so he could visit home. They couldn't tell me anything more. I felt like they had something to do with his secret box of photos, but I knew even less now I couldn't find them anywhere. I was convinced they would be here on his desk, open like they were before.

I stand around looking at the empty attic and desk and for a moment, I question whether those photos I had seen as a child even existed. I dangle the key to the attic in my hand. This is the last time I will be in here. My last time to check. The house will be sold and if I don't uncover its secrets now they will stay behind, buried in it. I drop the key onto the floor, and it rolls under the desk and against the floorboards. I kneel to pick it up and notice that the boards shift slightly. I grab the lamp and place it underneath the desk. These floorboards are not nailed down. They move slightly as my hands press the edges of them. I put the key back in my pocket and then drag the desk from its place, over to the side of the wall. Where the desk is, there are loose floorboards. I pull them up one by one.

Underneath them is a cavernous hole. Inside the hole, there is a chest. I heave it out of the hole into the light and open it up. Inside there is an old dress. I recognise it from the photographs. It is a Palestinian woman's dress; a *thobe*, embroidered with intricate stitches making symmetrical patterns over the chest piece, down to the hem. A different pattern of stitches adorns the arms. I run my fingers over the colourful threads. It is beautiful. I gently wrap it back up in the linen my dad had wrapped it in. Underneath the dress, there is a pile of scrapbooks. I count them out and lay them across the floor. There are twenty-two in total. Each one has one or two photographs in about halfway through. But other than a photo or two, they are empty. And right at the bottom of the chest, wrapped in a scrap of silk, is the photo of the girl.

At last, I have found her again. I hold her face up to the light and I feel once again that I am looking in a mirror and my childhood self is staring back. After all these years she now belongs to me. But who is she? I study the photograph. It couldn't have been me when I was younger because the photo is so old, and it was printed in black and white. But the resemblance is uncanny. I even had the same haircut as her when I was that age; the same fringe cut just below the eyebrows. She is standing in a garden, but I can't make much out in the background. I look at her face. She is smiling at me. There is mud smeared over a white dress and she is holding her hands up to the camera to show them to whoever is taking the picture. Would I know the person on the other side of the camera? Her eyes, I can't make out the colour, but they're looking straight through me as though for a split second, she can see me. Who is this girl and why is this all hidden away up here? I wrap the photograph in silk, but I keep this one with me. I don't want to lose her again. Now I have the photograph, I have some evidence that she was real, and she must mean something to me. I take the dress, the scrapbooks, and the photographs out of the attic. On my way down the ladder, I realise what my dad was trying to tell me before he died. They were underneath the desk. Buried. I understood now he was trying to tell me where to find them. He wanted me to have them. He wanted me to finish what he started, only I have no idea what that is. And I have no idea where to start searching.

***

The house is prepared for sale. I do not have any emotional attachment to it. The belongings that mean something to me have been taken out, but it was never the place I felt happy, or ever felt that my dad truly was. My most precious items from the house are the contents of the trunk. I have the *thobe* and the photographs, and they are now in my bedroom at the end of my bed. I want to keep them close and not hide them away in secret anymore.

I search the internet and find a *tatreez* group set up by an expert who now works at the Smithsonian Museum on the history and restoration of *tatreez* dresses. I contact her with some photos and the little information I have. My Tata was in her eighties when she passed, and it was a *thobe* from her childhood home in Jericho. That was all I could tell her.

The days pass in the hurried way that days pass after motherhood. They are days of routine, of school, cooking, and sleep. But since the photographs resurfaced my heart feels like it is split between two places. Each night I hold Hannah and Yousef a little closer. I remember the orphans. Sometimes when I close my eyes, they are being ripped away from me. Sometimes I imagine they are in the beds and the house is crumbling on top of us and I can't get them out from underneath the rubble. A jet plane tears through the sky, and I wonder if that is the last sound those I love will hear. My Palestinian stories are filtering into my present. I stay up late to write my stories, squeezing them into the small hours of the night when I have peace and my mind can go back and roam the streets there. They are my therapy; my exploration of trying to discover the world around me and how to impart that to my children.

It is early when I receive the email from Rania. I am sewing my own very basic cross-stitch pattern. I started it a while ago, but it isn't going well. Relieved, I tuck it away in my drawer and read the email instead. Rania tells me the dress was made over fifty years ago, but the designs are not typical of those from Jericho. They are more typical of the region around Al-Quds. It consists of traditional patterns but there are some fascinating stitches and tiles she hasn't seen before.

I run and fetch the *thobe* to look at the detail on it. I run my hand over the stitches and feel the fabric. As I examine the *tatreez*, I feel a bump under my fingers. I gently fold the dress so I can see the inside and try to find the bumps in the fabric. It feels as though it is a piece of paper. It is. It is an old piece of paper stitched to the inside of the dress by the front chest panel. It looks like a formal piece of paper. I shine my phone torch onto it. The writing is all in Arabic. I am trying to decipher the letters. I can make out our family name. Zaghari. I also read a short bit of writing underneath the Arabic word for city. It spells Deir Yassin.

Deir Yassin, Deir Yassin.

I knew the stories. They were carved into my mind. It was one of the most tragic events in Palestinian history. What I didn't know was anything about my family stories. They live miles away in Jericho. The climate is different. The fruits, the way of life. Is all of this not true? After all this time feeling connected, I am now in the dark. My Tata's *thobe*, from Al-Quds? I reread the email. 'A region of Al-Quds.' I search for Al-Quds and old maps of Palestine. Next to Al-Quds is the village of Deir Yassin.

Why would my Tata have a *thobe* from Al-Quds and official documents from Deir Yassin sewn into her dress? I root through the photographs once more and search the images for something other than the faces that I didn't know. But they are black and white, so they don't tell me much. They look rural, the setting. It doesn't look like a city or a place I have ever been to before. The one of the girl staring back at me makes me the most nervous because it is like staring at myself but of course, it couldn't have been me. None of it made any sense. The internet gave up nothing. The old names of the villages had been changed under the Israeli occupation. But there were some sites documenting its history before. I tried to see what I could find but it was all generic information. Nothing would tell me what it meant for me. For my family. If only Dad had told me.

I go back to my writing. My latest project is the hardest. I am writing about the daily life of those in Occupied Palestine. I speak to my family. Another cousin has been arrested. Another approaches his fifth year in jail. When I say I am British Palestinian to people I meet every day, either at school or through work, there is a pause while they process it. A pause where I can't imagine what runs through their head. I write my own narrative. I book work events. An upcoming live TV appearance for a local Islamic channel is due over the next couple of weeks for their evening show. They want to interview me, to talk to me about my newly published books and how it feels to write about Palestine.

I don't agree immediately. I am always wondering if they are my words to say. If they are ever my stories to tell. But the stories are part of a narrative the world rarely sees. A Palestine that is in my mind and inside the walls of my family houses. So, I agree to the set. Even though it is out of my comfort zone – all appearances are really – but it's the nature of my work after all. Whenever doubt creeps in, I remind myself that my family has it harder. They have to live with optimism and positivity under Occupation. There is an unwavering strength I see in their daily lives. It is a strength I wish I had inherited. What is an appearance on TV compared to a life under Occupation? A life I am always reminding myself that I don't live in. A life I dip in and out of. It is the half of me I think of. The half that was excluded from knowing about Deir Yassin. The half of me that doesn't speak Arabic so cannot be a part of everything because I can't understand what is being said. I am learning Arabic, but it doesn't come as easily as I would like. What happened in Deir Yassin that day? If I knew what I knew now, would I have even been brave enough to ask my dad?

I think about this on the train journey to the TV set. I hold my books in my hand and the photographs of my Tata and cousins are tucked inside my notebook. This will be the first time I speak about her since she and my dad passed away. I try to imagine her outside of the window through the trees of the blurred woodland but her memory fades from my mind's eye. The memory doesn't belong here. It is the wrong land for her.

'Come on, Layla, don't be shy. This is your home, your family.' I stand there as a child. It is a shock visit. One I was not prepared for because it was one I had not agreed to. A donkey was tied up outside, brought as a present for me to ride. I didn't want to do it. I felt like I should. So many expectant eyes watching me. 'Climb on, Layla, they brought it from our neighbour for you. He remembers you when you were very little, when you came with your mum.' I don't remember. As the donkey slowly meanders through the streets, I have a history lesson of who is who and who lives where. I look at the houses and as the neighbours hear the hum of the people, they come out and greet us and kiss us and offer us food. I couldn't understand why everyone was so welcoming and why they loved me. I wasn't from there. And it wasn't my home. It would take years before I understood that it was.

The set is ready, and I am invited to go on early and take photographs for social media before the filming starts.

I remember taking my first manuscript to the printers. I was a writer like thousands of others. For over five years I had worked on it and then I had left it in a drawer. Too scared to share something so intimate, yet felt like it wasn't my story to tell. And then I sent it out into the world. I had full manuscript requests from agents. I couldn't believe it. This never happened to debut novelists. Amidst the rejection letters, there were also replies! But as I ripped them open in anticipation or emailed them back and forth, my excitement turned into despondency. My only offers of publication included changing the character's ethnicity. I was told a British audience couldn't connect to my

Palestinian character. I thought of my cousins, alive, with life and hopes and dreams. I struggled to understand how connection differentiated humanity from one another. Maybe that was always the fight. Empathy. I carried the stack of freshly printed words that no one wanted. That was no hardship. No hardship at all, and so I borrowed their resilience even just for that moment and I carried on.

I wait outside the room as the cameras are busy setting up. As I wait, the recording room producer asks how to pronounce my surname a few times, so it won't be announced incorrectly on TV. I think again I should have kept my Palestinian maiden name so everyone would know who I was. But I move on. Was I ready? I say yes and move into the spot just outside of the cameras. There is a line I have to stay behind until I hear my name called. That is the cue for me to walk out on set. I pace to and fro. The cameraman waves his hand at me to stand behind the line. I worry everyone has seen my head popping into frame back and forth on their TV screens.

The presenter calls my name. I smile and take a deep breath as I walk out to the recorded sound of applause and sit comfortably in the bright armchair opposite her, making sure to cover my legs with my *abaya*. My books are on the table displayed for everyone to see. The presenter is effortless to talk to and so I relax. The lines I spent a while rehearsing on the way down allow me to have a smooth start, so I soon ease into it. They are displaying the photo of me with my Tata taken as a child. It flashes up on the TV screen, the one the audience sees at home. She asks me to tell her about the photo. I find myself telling her (and everyone watching the live show) that I had just found out that I wasn't a hundred percent sure anymore about where my Tata was from. I told them I had found a *thobe* in the attic, a piece of paper that mentioned our family name and the village of Deir Yassin alongside a collection of old photos. I didn't know who anyone in the photographs was. It was my own mystery that I couldn't solve.

The presenter knows the relevance of the village, Deir Yassin. It usually requires no further explanation. All I knew were the horror stories of that day. The orphans who were left behind in the Old City. I didn't know how my family were involved, and I had no idea how I was ever going to find out. *We hid under the dead animals.* I heard that in a story I was told about that day. They hid under the dead animals in the barn.

Girl.

I AM IN PARADISE. Thousands of miles away from home, I flew through the clouds to reach here. The azure, blue waves roll gently onto pristine white sands. A jungle backdrop of lush rainforest trees wraps around the coastline. There is nothing else ahead of me except for the ocean, vast and limitless. This is where I was going to find my purpose, my life.

Fatima.

Chapter 3

YEARS HAVE PASSED AND my memory takes me back to my childhood. I am older now. My mother is older but still looks as youthful as ever. My dad has returned from work covered in white powder; his hands are tough. They are accustomed to life as a stonemason. Along with my brothers, they are rebuilding our great-grandfather's house in the Old City. He and my brothers work later than usual, but it is summer; the days are longer, and we have light evenings.

It is wedding season. The town is strewn with banners and lights from tree to tree and in between the house and garden of the bride. I am there with Mama and Lulu and our neighbours from next door come out to meet us on the porch. I take Suad's hand and run into the crowd. Her mother is already there; she is singing and dancing with the women as they celebrate our neighbour's wedding. She pulls Suad's hand and in turn mine, deeper into the crowd. We are surrounded by clapping and music until we are all worn out and the bride encourages us all to rest and go to her grandfather's gardens for food. After nibbling at some of the food, Suad and I steal off into the fields surrounding the houses and sit underneath the trees as the lights of the city twinkle below us.

'Do you think you will get married one day?' I ask her.

She giggles. 'I am going to marry Mahmoud, the stonecutter's son in my class.'

I laugh with her.

'You?'

I am too shy to answer but she already knows. 'I know who it will be. You will marry Kareem!'

I laugh but don't answer. Inside I wonder how it will feel to be older and more beautiful just like my sister. I think that is who I will be like when I grow up.

'I want to be a teacher,' Suad says.

'I already know what I want to be when I grow up. A stonemason like my dad.'

Suad bursts out laughing. 'You can't be a stonemason!'

'Why not?'

'You are a girl! Anyway, come on, young girl with crazy dreams, all this talk of getting older is making me hungry again.'

We skip hand in hand back to the party and eat more of the food, staying up until our bodies give in to the sweet slumber of sleep in the gardens as others begin to clear up around us. Drifting in and out of sleep, I dream I am working with the stone just like my baba. He can teach me. I could learn to cut it and build houses, maybe even bigger buildings like mosques or schools. I can't describe, even to my best friend, how I love the feel of stone underneath my fingertips. How it is cut from the quarry then shaped and chiselled to form part of history that over time will become ancient and perhaps have generations of people running their hands over its surface, many years from now. How it is made of the bodies of millions of sea creatures that existed even before the dinosaurs. I could cut patterns in the stone. The patterns merge with my mama's *tatreez* patterns. I could cut the stone that way and use it as my own signature, my own mark on history. I can do it and I am going to prove it. I am going to start tomorrow with the tools my baba has at home. I will show Suad just how talented I am. It runs in our family. It runs through our blood.

As the sun rises and wakes me up, I head back to my house and fetch Baba's tool bag. I take it around the side of the house and begin chipping at the stone. My hands work clumsily. The stone chips and falls in a lump by my feet. I move to another piece, gentler this time, starting at the edge. I make a simpler pattern I have seen my mama sew. It is a zig-zag in the embroidery of her *thobe*. It is one of her favourites. It represents eternity. I begin bit by bit, denting the stone to make a zig-zag pattern across the stone on the wall of our home. Eternity. It will last forever.

I am interrupted by Baba calling my name. I drop his tools and run towards him until he picks me up and swings me in the air. '*Salam*, Baba, I have been working as hard as you.'

'Is that so?'

'Yes and look what I have created!'

'Wow, the stonemason's daughter is just as skilled! I was wondering where my tool bag had gone. Why don't you come with me to Grandpa's house, and you can help me restore it?'

'Really, Baba, you mean it?'

'Why not? I could do with some help.'

'Can we go today?'

'No, my darling, we can't. I have a meeting with the neighbouring towns,' he sighs deeply.

'What about?'

'An agreement between us, to keep the peace.'

'But we see them and have dinner with them all the time.'

He smiles at me and ruffles my hair. He doesn't say anything else. He just carries me inside our house, warm and smelling of roasted chicken, onions, and the almonds I picked a few days ago off our almond trees.

Layla.

Chapter 3

I AM GLAD I did the show. It always feels logistically hard to organise with the children and I find it hard to separate my home life from work, but whenever I participate in an event, I feel like I've accomplished something. I try to keep positive; you never know who is watching, or who might learn something.

However, what I didn't expect is what happened next. There I am in the middle of an ordinary day, cooking dinner, the house busy after a day at school for the children, my work fading into the background of everyday life. And there it is. An email in my inbox after my appearance on the show. I scan it, not expecting much, and then I have to sit down. I reread it. It is from a film director. It is a succinct email. They are researching for potential candidates to take part in a history programme for a major broadcaster in the UK about their links to their British Palestinian heritage. He thinks it might help unravel my family secret. Would I be interested and agree to a phone call?

I am nervous because it reminds me of something I asked for over a decade ago. I had prayed one night during Ramadan, asking for the opportunity to return to Palestine with a TV crew so I could show the world what I knew of it. Can it be that after all this time it is coming true? I had long forgotten my lofty ambitions as a young woman. I didn't really want them anymore; I was far more content to be lesser known, to live my life away from the glare and critique of others. But I remember the night I asked for it, as if all those years had not passed and it was merely the night before. I remember it with so much clarity that I am sure, deep down in my heart, despite the odds of it happening, this opportunity is meant for me.

I agree to the phone call and after the first call, there are many more. He mentions that they might be able to discover something about my Tata's childhood, but they need a lot of information to see if they can make a factual story from our family history. From family names, dates of birth, places of birth, and marriages. Over the next few weeks, they collate the information from the scraps I give them. I realise I know very little about my family heritage when it comes to dates and names of great-grandparents, etc. They investigate in the archives, using the national documents and historical data they have access to. They are searching to find out if and how we are linked to 1948 Palestine.

What will they find? I am sceptical that there won't be much left of fact and truth. But if they do find anything I will only find out on camera. It isn't an easy choice. But if I have a chance of finding out what happened in the past that my dad was too afraid to tell me, I must take it. And what about my Tata? She wanted us to find out, at least, I think that's what my dad meant about fulfilling her last wish. And the girl in the photograph. Who was she? And why does she look so much like me?

In the weeks that follow I am on edge, wondering what will come of this. I am uncomfortable about what they may discover. Perhaps there is a reason no one has told me before. Perhaps there is a reason they don't want the ghosts of their pasts dragged into the present, where they don't belong. I can't even ask Tata because she isn't here anymore. Her stories are not written down. Not many in her generation wrote down their history. It is captured in other ways. Whoever owns history, owns the future. I will find out that Tata could not have written even if she had wanted to.

The team calls me. They have found the truth hidden away in archives, in old maps, and work done by historians and archaeologists. The director asks if we can meet. It is the next formal step. Another step closer. If I am not chosen, I will not discover any more than I already know. With it so close, almost in reach, I am starting to imagine what it will be like to have answers. Maybe he wants to meet to see how I will fare on TV? Not that anyone can fully predict it. I mean, I thought nothing could be harder than live TV, right? If it went wrong, there was nowhere to hide. This at least wasn't live. But friendly interviews and book promotion tours are in a completely different category to this. I must learn to separate this. This isn't about my books or even me. It is about discovering what happened to my family, for my father and his last dying wish. It is one thing to discover it, another thing to discover it on live TV, and quite another to have it revealed piece by piece and edited by someone else into a film to be shown to the public. Is this what I really want?

I arrange for us to meet just outside of the village at a rural centre close to home. My childhood home for the longest part of it was now just down the road but it is empty, so I don't visit. There is no one there anymore.

I have a few moments to gather my thoughts and reflect on the fact that decades later I am back here in my childhood village, meeting a director about participating in a film about Palestine. It feels so far away from my life here, especially my childhood. I didn't think about it much then. But children don't. Your life is the here and now. For most of my childhood and throughout my teens, I lived in England with my British mother, and although I knew my surname and heritage were different, as a child it didn't matter except for the occasional time I was reminded of it. I didn't go through my childhood feeling particularly different. But there were some exceptions I remember, like when my sister changed her surname to my mother's British name so hers wouldn't stand out. Like the time we said our dad was Spanish. Or the time we hid that we had lived in Arabia once. Or when people asked, where was I really from? I was born in the local hospital twenty minutes' drive away, so I never fully understood what that meant.

I walk through the grounds contemplating how I will decide to go ahead or not. The working farm in the distance is now just a farmhouse with cattle in the back field. I look out over the fences into the expanses of countryside and wonder how I ended up back here after all this time. I travelled so far away, and yet this place was like a boomerang pulling me back again.

I wander back inside and sit at a quiet table with my notebook out. I want to make sure I don't forget anything, just in case I am picked. Picked? Selected? I am not sure what the deal is so I am also terrified of what I might represent and how I might come across. What they discover could change everything. Am I ready for that? Are the children and my husband? Can I really trust this production company to represent Palestine sensitively and authentically? My past experiences have taught me to be cautious. But I realise that this doesn't matter now because the chances of being selected (despite my prayers) are one of many. It is a long shot. Outside the window someone with a leather bag and a notebook is looking through the windows; not your usual customer around here. It is the director and I wave to him so he can see me.

After the greetings are out the way and breakfast is brought over (he had a long drive from visiting someone else for the film), we begin. I understand his angle; it is about storytelling on a personal basis, not about the political Palestine that is usually reported in the news. This will focus on family stories. He will tell the history of my grandmother and her mother and our family. The research team uses historical evidence to piece together the past. He has been through this process many times before with other programming on discovering family heritages. He stresses that it isn't always possible to find out the truth. They are working on it as we speak, and he hopes that the last pieces of the puzzle come together so he has something to tell me. My heart drops a bit. I express my concerns about finding historical facts under an Occupation that is continually erasing, even in the present. He agrees it will be difficult. But not impossible. I tell him my fears, that the final edit needs to be fair and representative. He assures me it will be. Can I ask for things to be removed or edited if I don't like them? No, he is quite clear on that. It will be up to him and the production team to direct it for the public. I have to trust him. This is the bit that makes me nervous. I spend a few moments making notes in my book. As I ponder on the issues at stake, I realise no one can make me say anything I don't want to on camera. I also have enough experience now to know the potential problem areas and stereotypes that could be positioned. Maybe I am a bit naïve, but what is my alternative? To say no to this opportunity?

I ask about wardrobe planning, film schedules, and dates. If I am chosen, the filming will begin in the summer in the UK and then I'll be off to Palestine afterwards. If I am chosen. He reiterates that bit. I tell him I think I want it. I feel as though I can't let this opportunity pass me by. This feeling grows throughout the meeting. He has contacted my family in Jericho. They are on board and happy to help with whatever information he needs. Knowing that they are happy with it makes me feel better too. After all, it is as much their story as it is mine. So, I agree. If they choose me, I will return home to Palestine.

***

A couple of weeks pass after we meet when he calls me. His number flashes up on the screen and I am on my own at home. I sit on the sofa and take a deep breath before I answer. At this stage, I have an idea of what he is going to say, but the way my heart beats knowing how much I am now invested in this, I know I will be gutted if it isn't me; if it isn't us, or our family.

I answer. I have been selected to take part in the show. They have pieced together my family's history back to 1948.

'We have discovered your Tata's past,' he says. 'It is water-tight. No one can argue with it.'

The next couple of weeks I am inundated with emails and contracts I have to sign. I am increasingly aware of how invested everyone is after this moment. Itineraries are booked, passports are organised, and producer phone calls happen. It is actually happening. It is coming together so quickly that I don't have any more time for contemplation. I am going to find out whether I am ready or not.

***

The recording morning arrives with an early knock at the door from the TV crew. The first part of the interview is going to be filmed in my dining room with a casual chat and introduction to the viewers about the setup: I am searching for the truth about my Tata's past. They will take me on a journey to find out what happened to her. My husband takes the children to school but they are excited about being on TV, so they don't leave until they agree with the film crew to get some shots of them when they get back. It is going to be a full day of filming.

As they are busy setting up, I go around our neighbour's house to explain what is happening in case they are interrupted by the TV crew vans and people being filmed up and down our street.

'Is it for a crime documentary?' they ask.

I laugh. That was their first thought?

'No, nothing like that, just a history documentary. They are filming so you might see the drone capturing the street and the fields, and a car driving up and down being filmed.'

'Ooh, how exciting. Will it just be for today?'

'The rest of the filming will be in Palestine,' I say. It hasn't sunk in. I will be filming in Palestine next month.

The car the presenter arrives in pulls up outside as the crew records her. This is my excuse to leave my neighbour's doorstep and get back inside to answer the door. I put my shoes on. Although I wouldn't usually be wearing sandals casually in the house, I feel underdressed to be in bare feet or socks. I brush down my dress and adjust my scarf. I am behind the door, waiting for them to knock.

They film me opening the door and inviting the presenter in. She is a Palestinian actress who lives in London. She has her own heritage links that they are also exploring as part of the film.

I invite her in, trying not to sound too staged, which I find almost impossible with cameras behind us, in front of us, and to the side of us. Do I shake her hand? Is that too formal? We do the greeting a handful of times before they are happy with it. Then we move on to the next stage. The interview.

We walk into the kitchen, and she asks me questions to get to know me a bit more. I try to answer naturally but it is harder than I realise with a room full of people, cameras, and microphone packs tucked into my clothes. I make tea, many times. She asks about my childhood and growing up. 'Did you know any Palestinians?' she says as she leans against the fridge, while I reach for more teabags from the cupboard.

'None, actually.' I realise for the first time I had grown up quite separately from the other part of me.

'Me neither. Well, now we have met,' she says warmly, as we move over to the table with the fifth cup of tea I have now made for the camera shots. The photographs of Tata are on the table. She points to the one of her smiling. 'What can you tell me about her?'

'I just remember her being central to the home. Cooking for us, smiling, wearing her *thobes*. That's a great photo actually as it's how I remember her.'

'What would you say to her if she was here?'

'I would tell her that she could confide in me about anything. That I feel guilty that I didn't know anything about her life when she was young. I'd ask her what happened, who the photographs are of.'

'Where would you go to find out these answers now that she isn't here?'

'The natural place to start would be the family farm in Jericho. My family is still there.'

'Then that's where we will go to next.'

In the month that follows the team prepare for us to leave. It is a five-day filming schedule that begins the moment I arrive at the land border crossing in Amman, Jordan. It is also the typical route my family would have taken so it made sense we mirrored their journey. I remember my dad's tickets. The ones he booked for us from here to Amman. I feel a sense of relief that I am making the journey he wanted; just not in the way either of us would have imagined.

I arrive at Amman International Airport and a VIP service collects me from the arrivals hall. They whisk me through passport control and out to a private taxi that takes me to the Amman Airport Hotel. It is 2am so I am relieved I can have a few hours' rest before my 7am pick-up the next day. I cannot sleep. My mind is racing.

The taxi picks me up early as planned and drives towards the land crossing at Amman. The plan is to film me entering Palestine through the border. The company has agreed with Israeli security to close the VIP section of the crossing for an hour to allow us to film. It is an experience I have never been a part of in real life before because Palestinians always travel through the Palestinian side. The Palestinian side includes a bustling hall, long queues, and invasive questioning. The VIP route is significantly different. A filmed VIP route is even more so. I walk through the hall. It is empty and around me, security waits with smiling faces. An Israeli security guard beams, 'Welcome.'

I stop in my tracks, and we have to reshoot. 'Sorry,' I say. I didn't expect that.

I am not sure which part of this arrivals recording will be used in the film. It is a lot of responsibility to represent Palestinians on film in a modern-day context, especially because I am haunted by this feeling of only being half-Palestinian, because I have a British mother and a passport which means I enter and leave in different ways. I have spent a decade writing about my family experiences because I don't feel the world gets to see the true Palestine. I am now standing in the country wondering if even I do. I can't capture their experience and it troubles me.

'How do you feel about being back in Palestine?'

I look into the film lens repeating different answers. 'It feels great. I am glad to be back. I'm home.' But they all sound wooden, contrived. 'Let's just keep this scene quiet,' the director says. I agree. I am exposed on a film that will be broadcast to everyone and I am not telling the truth. I want to say I wouldn't enter this way. I would be on the Palestinian side. I would be nervous about whether they would even let me in, especially since all my work has been about Palestine for the last decade. I wonder if they would restrict my movements to the West Bank or stop me from entering completely. I am uncomfortable about this filming. I don't want to construct this narrative. It isn't real. I feel like a Palestinian poster child for an Israeli tourist video. The director agrees with me, and we leave the airport. As the Mercedes taxi drives off, I am relieved. We have entered the country at least. If we hadn't, it would be over before it even started. But we are in. We can put it behind us and carry on doing what we are here to do; finding out what secrets have been hiding in the dark for an entire lifetime.

***

The accommodation is in Jerusalem. In the flurry of emails between being selected and arriving, there was one where they asked what part of Jerusalem I would feel most comfortable in. The truth is I didn't know. I'd never stayed in Palestine unless it was with my family in their homes. So I agree to any part of Jerusalem. As I walk into the dated hotel room in the Jewish Quarter of Jerusalem, I wish I had requested somewhere else. One of the positives is that it is a ten to fifteen-minute walk to the Old City. Since that is all I want from my Jerusalem stay, I don't ask to be moved. Plus, I'm only going to be here for five days. I can handle five days, right?

I check into my room and ask reception how to get to Al-Aqsa. The instructions are simple. We are close. I turn left and walk straight down the hill, all the way until I reach the gates of the Old City. Down the hill, there is a park to my left with a stage set up for a music festival that I am to overhear that evening. Later, a Palestinian taxi driver tells me that it is a cemetery and some of the Prophet's (peace be upon him) companions are buried there. I am saddened by the disrespectfulness of it.

Across the road, an archway leads to a shopping centre. The entire newly built strip is built in the ancient limestone of the city. The strip is made of luxury shops, high street shops, and perfume shops. There is a poster of a barely dressed model in the window. She covers her chest with her arms and behind her, up some steps, the Old City comes into view. It is an odd introduction to one of the holiest cities in the world. A shopping district, racy advertisements, and pop music, and then across the road, the walls of the historic city. I remember reading about cases of 'Jerusalem Syndrome' where religious devotees couldn't come to terms with the fact that Jerusalem was a modern city. They arrived here and were sent mad, believing they were prophets or sent on a divine mission to do something in the city. It was a condition so specific to Jerusalem (hence its name) that it had never been reported anywhere else in the world. I reach out and touch the limestone. I remember my boys telling me how it is made of prehistoric sea creatures. Is everything we build, built on the death of something else?

As I approach the Old City, I see a Palestinian stonemason working on the restoration of the walls around it. He has a tool bag around his waist, and he is working with hammers and chisels. He is covered in powder that looks like snow. The modern shops in the Jewish Quarter are built of the same stone, the same stone that continues to build the city. Generations lost and yet the continuity of the stone constructs its authenticity.

Many families we know have stonemasons in their family. Not as many now, of course, but before. They told me they see them stealing the stones from the ruined villages. They steal them and rebuild them somewhere else. The carbon dating faking its history. The ongoing Occupation is built on the stolen bricks of others. The hands building the stone and the Palestinians behind it remain under threat, but still, their belts are on, and they are building.

'Where is the stone from?' I ask. He points to the top of the hill. I know where he is pointing to.

I leave him working and walk through the Old City gate. The entryway is cool and damp, lined with delicious locally grown melons, oranges, cucumbers, tomatoes, figs, and dates. The produce looks and smells amazing. I can't resist handing over sheikals in return for sliced figs and oranges. It is the best food I have ever tasted.

I meander through the city, already bustling with trade, tourists, pilgrims and locals weaving in and out of the stalls. I follow the occasional sign that leads me to the heart of the city. The ancient walls tower above each side of me and when my eyes glance upwards, I can see people's homes and court-yards. And then I hear it; the call to prayer rings out through the winding streets. A glimpse of the gold on the Dome of the Rock, the courtyard, a wide inviting space after the twists and turns of the *souk*'s streets. I pass by the Dome of the Rock, its gold dome roof glinting in the sun. I take the steps down to Al-Aqsa Mosque and place my sandals in the rack. I feel calmer. If this was all the trip was for, it was worth it. It is a privilege to be here, and it is a place many never get the oppor-tunity to visit. I spend some time on the rich red carpet after making my prayers. I look up to its ornate ceiling and the history contained within its walls. I wish my children were here. Next time, *Insha'Allah*.

I make it back to my room before dusk. I plan to sleep early because filming starts at seven in the morning. According to the schedule, tomorrow's filming and each subsequent day after that won't finish until the evening, and that's if everything goes smoothly. I try to sleep but I can't. I toss and turn, wondering what tomorrow will reveal. My unease is heightened by the fact that I am staying in the middle of Jerusalem. I can't shift the feeling that I don't belong here. I remember my dad telling me our family used to own land and property throughout Jerusalem. He used to own so much of Jerusalem, before.

Since I can't sleep, I walk down to the late-night café. It is just me in the café, but the streets outside are busy with people walking up and down, cars honking, and lights shining into the windows. I call home to check in on my husband and children. The children are asleep. I miss their voices. My husband tells me they are all fine. It won't be long until I see them again, he says. I say goodbye as I see the film crew arriving back from a late dinner. They are laughing and joking together. I ask how dinner was. They tell me they had *maklouba* at an Israeli restaurant, and it was delicious. My stomach turns. That is a Palestinian dish, I tell them.

Tourists mill in and out. Everyone is greeted here from all over the world, and they come for its wonders, its stories, its religions. Shortly after, I go to my room. I barely sleep but when I do I dream of ransacked villages and a new normal where I don't feel welcome in my father's homeland.

I dress early and go to the breakfast hall. No one particularly pays attention to me, but I stand out in this room. It is a standard hotel room with a decent buffet for breakfast, but I feel different here. There are no Palestinians; that much is obvious. I sit at a table on the back wall and scan the film schedule. There is the start time, a lunch break factored in, and a couple of location changes. That is all I have. They don't give me any more information because there needs to be dramatic storytelling on film. I understand that, but still, it isn't a good feeling that everyone else knows what is coming and I don't. I can barely eat. My stomach is writhing under my clothes and my hands are clammy. I have some watermelon (which I fancied since seeing it sliced up at the Old City), but I can't manage anything else.

I go back up to my room and check the time. It is time to meet at the crew van. I check my face. It is powdered and I am using highlighters to erase the bags under my eyes. I go down to the café where I have a view of the streets. The crew van is there; a large nine-seater in a dull matte black with tinted windows. Some other members of the team are there. An Israeli fixer and a Palestinian cameraman who I later learn will also be our translator. The director walks in and stops when he spots me. He has been looking for me.

'You will travel behind us in the taxi for the first scenes. I want to capture you arriving in the taxi and driving through Jericho. Are you okay with that? Are you comfortable doing that if we are right behind you?'

'Yes, sure, just give me a minute. I need to grab some water.'

I go back up to my room and throw up. I can't do this. I take deep breaths and try to steady my nerves. Why did I agree to this? My mind works frantically, trying to work out how to avoid it. I think of the months of planning. The flights. The logistics. I remember Tata. I am here to find out what happened to my family. I have to do this, or I may never discover what happened. I am in shock that I don't know already and yet I really believed I did. Why wouldn't I? Why wouldn't I have believed that she was from Jericho and spent a happy life there? With all the history I know about Palestine right up to its present, I am sick again. How naïve have I been?

I check the time on my phone. I have only been five or so minutes. I can go down and they won't have a clue that I am losing it. I need to pull it together. I think of my cousins and how excited they are to be part of this. I think of their brothers in jail. They live with this and here I am on a film production, and I can't even manage that. I can do this. I have people expecting me to do this.

I sip cold water and check my reflection in the mirror. I look presentable. The first location is Jericho. I will be with my family today and I haven't seen them in years. I imagine this. Home to my family. This is what gets me through. Before I go downstairs into the lobby, I pack a spare plastic bag in my handbag with lip balm, powder, and paracetamol – my survival kit for the day. I pull my face into a smile whilst breathing deeply into my lungs to steady my nerves. I check I have the photograph of the girl with me. Today, I will ask my family who she is. I push the button in the lift. People are heading out for a day of sightseeing. I am envious that they have such a simple day planned. I go outside to the director and I meet the taxi driver; a Palestinian from a village that no longer exists. He tells me about it on the drive and I am transported there, away from the present.

Soon the cityscape changes. We drive down through the roads cut out in the side of the mountains. Down we spiral, away from the mountainous sand dunes. An old mosque is hidden by palm trees, tucked away on the roadside. I wonder if I can take a few minutes out and go and pray in the serene prayer hall. I don't ask. I know it isn't possible. We pull up and the crew, having arrived before us, are setting up the cameras in a layby by the side of the sandy road.

I wind my window down as the director approaches.

'We are almost ready to start filming. We will count down on the handheld radio,' he says, passing it to the driver. 'We will communicate with this.' He walks around to my window.

'Okay, Layla, we are going to film this as part of your arrival in Jericho. All you have to do is look out the window and keep it rolled down.'

I nod my head. I can actually manage that and probably only that right now, so this is a good thing.

'Take off your sunglasses though. Be good to get a shot of your face without them on.'

I take them off, ready.

The cameras start rolling. The countdown from five comes in through the handheld to the taxi driver. He begins to drive. I look out of the window of the taxi as the familiar scenery of Jericho whisks past the windows. It is the land outside of the town and it is mostly sand dunes. A highway runs past in the distance that connects the town. Just down that road will be the same balmy hot air, the streets lined with palm trees, and my Tata's home. Or was it? An undercurrent of anxiety runs through me as I realise the world I have been busy writing about will soon be ripped out from under my feet.

'Are you okay?' the taxi driver asks.

'Yes, why?' I reply, relieved to have my thoughts broken momentarily.

'Do you have asthma?'

'No, why?' I am wondering if he asks because of the sandy desert air blowing in through the open window.

'It's just you are breathing like you have asthma.'

'*Alhamdulillah*, I am okay, *shukran*.'

I am not okay, but I am past being able to do anything about it. I have no choice but to go through the process now. The instructions come through the handheld radio. We are stopping and starting, driving down the road, pulling over to let the quarry trucks pass whenever they appear from behind the dunes. They might be able to close the airport, but we have to be patient on the roads. Then we go again, hoping for a clear run so we can catch the shot. We are going to start filming again in three-two-one. We drive back and forth until all the scenes are captured.

'I think I am the star of this film,' the taxi driver jokes.

I am glad he is.

'We have it. Thanks, turn around, and let's just take one more and then we can head to Jericho,' the voice says via the radio.

For the next part of the filming, the sound guy and the director come with me in the taxi and film the shots from inside the car. Now it is time to drive to the centre of Jericho. The first place I would naturally look for answers is back on the farm with my family. My uncle, my dad's brother, lives there with my aunty and their five children; my cousins. The familiar town of my childhood comes into view. I remember its streets so well: the petrol station before we drive in, the stalls with beach inflatables, the winds in the roads, the turning off to the cable car, and Temptation Mount. Perhaps because I have spent my adult life writing about it and reminding myself of it, so I don't forget. Capturing each and every minute detail before it changes. In case I lose it, or it is taken. But this time, as I drive through, I am wondering how different my family's home is. Jericho is a landscape unlike any other in the West Bank and Palestine. Palestine is so diverse in its landscapes and terrains. In what fruit grows where, in how livelihoods are made. The *tatreez* patterns on the dresses, even the cut of the dresses depending on the region, are so different. I wonder if I have missed any of these clues in my Tata's life. Had I missed things about her that would have given away her childhood and her past?

'Why did no one tell me?' I say, realising I had said it out loud and my microphone picked it up.

'It is quite common for families not to share their history. And if you aren't a history buff, it isn't something you discover. We experience it a lot doing these shows.'

It makes sense. Why would anyone want to bring it up, and how could you to a child, and then a young idealistic adult? Is it something you mention over family dinners in the courtyard at night? Then the feeling of dread resurfaces like acid in my stomach. If no one has spoken about it, maybe they don't want to and here I am, about to ask.

The taxi drives down the street of the farmhouse. I instinctively recognise this street despite how long I have been away from it. It is the same street I see when I am miles away from here, the most important one to me in Ariyha. There is a shop at the top of the street just after a steep turn down a hill. A patch of unused, overgrown farmland to the left, and then just past it, stone walls and a gate that leads to my family's courtyard. It has been years. I have dreamt of being back here. But life got in the way.

I see my aunty standing there in the courtyard, dressing the table, her eyebrows gently furrowed as she concentrates on the task at hand. My cousins mill about the doorway, with freshly made-up faces and new hijab scarfs pinned perfectly around their necks. I jump out of the taxi as soon as it pulls up. Finally, the feeling in the pit of my stomach disappears and for the first time on the trip, a weight lifts and is replaced with a buzz of happiness.

'Aunty, *salam alaikom*,' I say and throw my arms around her. I can't help it. At last, a feeling I recognise. I am safe with her. We speak and kiss each other, she holds me back and pinches my cheeks. I apologise for not coming back. But it doesn't matter now because in this moment I am with her again. She is always there, calmly running the house with a sweet smile on her face, one that doesn't give away how tirelessly she works for the family and her five children. She looks almost the same as she did during my childhood, just as youthful; her skin clear with a gentle smattering of freckles across the bridge of her nose. 'I've missed you,' I say, and it is true. I finally relax. This is my Palestine.

'We got it, we got the whole thing recorded. Brilliant entrance. We couldn't have staged it better!' the film crew says, entering through the gate behind us with their equipment bags, ready to set up. They had all been there before, met the family, and decided where to film and shoot. Everyone knew what to expect, everyone except me.

'Where do you want me?' I say.

'We will call you when we have set up. It shouldn't take long.'

I find my aunty and uncle in the kitchen as the crew prepares the front room. They tell me how good it is to see me and how they wish the children could have come. I pull out the photograph. I am more nervous than I imagined.

'Do you know who this is?'

'Where did you find it?' my uncle asks.

'It was with Dad's belongings,' I answer, my fingers trembling slightly on the corners of the photo.

I watch my uncle as he studies it. My aunty too. Her face creases up.

'It looks like one of your great aunts to me.'

'No, that looks like it could it be Tata Suad.'

'Or even her sister?'

'I can't tell.'

I must have given the disappointment away in my face.

'I am sorry, *habibte*. It is so hard to know for sure. It looks like it was taken a long time ago and *Masha'Allah* you look so similar, it could even be you!' my aunt says, consoling me.

I smile to hide my disappointment. The TV crew calls them to the lounge. 'Can we set up your microphones now?'

They leave and I go and see my cousins in the middle room and leave the crew to it. My cousins hug me and laugh at my red cheeks from the Jericho heat.

'I know, I know, I am so bad in the heat. I was worried when they said they were filming in the summer.'

'Last week was even hotter, so you should be relieved!' Amira laughs, powdering my cheeks with the kit I brought with me. 'All of us have been waiting for you. You look so beautiful.'

'No, I definitely don't. I have felt sick all morning!'

'Why?'

'I don't know, just being on camera.'

'Look at us, all dressed and ready. I hear the director is giving Mama a microphone and she hates to be the centre of attention, yet here we are waiting to be asked and no one asks us!'

'I don't know what they are going to ask.'

'Us too, but we find out soon.'

'For Tata, for Tata.'

Tata is not here. We are in the room she used to sleep in. Her absence echoes around the house. The bed she was laid up in is gone. An integral member of the family is no longer with us. I look around as the girls re-pin my scarf like pros. Amira is pinning it to my shoulder whilst Sumaya frames my face first and tucks my flyaway hair back. They are busy fussing as I look at the empty space. I remember her warm face, smiling, her row of white teeth, and her long dark hair. How she always wore *thobes*. She liked dark colours with handmade embroidery on heavily decorated chest panels, much like the one I found. It was hanging in my wardrobe back home. I had kept the linen on it but hung it to preserve the fabric. When I touched the fabric, it reminded me of sitting on her lap as a young child whilst the lilies grew around our feet. Since my emails with Rania, I had begun researching the ancient patterns stitched into the dress, *tatreez*, now a UNESCO-listed heritage in the preservation of Palestinian culture. They found similar patterns dating back to the 5th century on the bodies of buried infant girls, known as the Qadisha Valley mummies. I don't stop to imagine why they had been buried in their best dresses. Their dresses, layer upon layer of them, are now removed from their tiny bodies and displayed in museums. I shake off the thought and come back into the room, in the present, with my young vibrant cousins fussing around me. I am still so uncomfortable being filmed but I realise I am here for all of us. We need to know what happened that day and so does the world. This could be the one opportunity I have in my entire life to do this. And to find out what my dad kept from me and what he promised my Tata. It is a heavy weight to take on my shoulders, but being with them all made me realise I am not alone. It is not just mine to bear.

Fatima.
Chapter 4

THE SUN BREAKS IN shards through my window. The light is split between the stone before it enters my bedroom. It warms my eyelids and brings me into the present. I try to move my body but it doesn't want to move yet, so I lay still. I know the time by the rays, and I feel a pang of guilt as I realise I have slept through the dawn prayer. I am no longer woken by the *athan* echoing out of the minaret and reverberating through the stone alleyway and through the holes in my window. I will be there soon, I imagine. Far, far above the clouds and *Insha'Allah* into paradise. It makes my body move, slowly to the washbowl, so I can prepare. I pray *fajr*. My heart is at peace. Footsteps and the sound of the wooden wheels of market carts begin on the cobbles outside the window. The world is waking up and today I must find the vigour to feel alive and part of it because today is the day the film crew arrives. My sons are visiting from America. She is coming. Today is the start of the end.

I dress in my favourite *thobe*. It is the only one I have from my mama. She made many, but lots of them were sold to make ends meet. After it happened, she wasn't the same again. I would find her weeping from morning to night. Our neighbours tell me she will recover. It will just take time. But time passed and she could only manage less. I took over for her, allowing her body to rest. Allowing her eyes to close and wander off, to go to a place to be with them.

When she slept, I ran away to the streets. I heard of the orphans that were found at the gates and I am sure Lulu will be there. Every day, with no shoes on my feet, because that was another thing we had left behind. There was no money for new sandals. I ran through the unfamiliar Old City Streets, lost in its maze-like alleyways that wound around the town. I am at the church they had been seen at, but they aren't here now.

Days pass and finally, I find the house of Hind. She lets me in. I run up the stairs of her grandfather's mansion and scour every room, shouting for the children to turn around so I can see their faces, to make sure she isn't there. Maybe Lulu is taking care of them, maybe she forgot she has a family. Maybe that was where she wanted to teach so she had stayed with Hind.

Every day I went back so the possibility of seeing her wouldn't fade. It was possible. Things like this happened all the time, where family members were separated, sometimes for months, even years, and then miraculously one day they would find them. I had heard stories about that happening. It meant I had a purpose. I had something to do that could make everything right.

But as time passed, I felt differently going up the stairs and seeing the children. Sometimes I stayed with them for a while. Sometimes I would just wander through the city, through its secret caves and its network of hiding spaces, searching for a teenage girl with honey-coloured hair who was missing. I knew she was angry with me but that made me all the more determined to find her, to apologise. to beg her to come home. She mustn't stay away simply because she was upset with me. Mama was missing her, and she was heartbroken after losing Baba and her sons. She had to come back to stop causing us more pain.

I walk home and I can hear screaming from the rooms upstairs. It is my mama. I run up the stairwell, terrified of what I will find behind the old door. She grabs me and hugs me before pushing me away. She demands to know where I went. I went to find Lulu. She is silent. I went to find Lulu.

She shouts at me and tells me to stop listening to stories. I am banned from roaming the streets. It is too dangerous. It isn't safe for a girl of my age to be out there, wandering around. I could be snatched from the streets or put in one of the orphanages. Have I seen them? They are now full of Yassini girls.

I cry. Just as I did that day. And from that moment, after I see my mother in that much pain, I stop. I stop seeking Lulu and my brothers. I never mention my baba. I stop my carvings on stone. The stone-cutting plant is still there. It is ours. I won't forget. I will just wait a while. There is talk of going back one day. I hear them talk about it. Time will pass and we will return. She was adamant about returning. It belonged to us after all. She had seen my baba build it from nothing.

But what I am shy to tell her is that I don't know if I want to go back. What if they come again when we go back? What if I see the quarry and I can't breathe? What if I can't live in the house where we all lived because it reminds me every day of what I have lost? I glance up towards the hills out of the Old City and in the distance, I know that is Deir Yassin. As the days pass and that day replays itself in my memory, I panic.

My mind turns black and red, and fear engulfs me like poisonous smoke, and I have to sit down with my head between my knees. I can't breathe. 'Are you okay?' my mama asks as I struggle to catch my breath. She doesn't know what to do so she leaves me. She can't watch another child die.

I am calm now. I survived. It only happens when I look up there, so I stop looking. I stop thinking of it. Instead, I explore the streets. They are city streets so different to before, but their difference is good for me now. They are hard stone streets, there are no fields, no almond trees. I pass my time by sitting with my mama and stitching.

I am outside one day sitting on the street as the light is better than in the stone house. A woman walks past. She has a strong figure, slender but with broad shoulders, and she is wearing clothes I haven't seen before. I think she is a traveller passing through. She sees me working on the dress. I have almost finished it. 'How much?' she says, and she takes it from my fingers, inspecting the handiwork my mama has spent hours and hours on. I shrug my shoulders. It isn't for sale; it is for Mama to wear. But my mind works fast. She has nowhere to wear the dress. She has one for here, the house she rarely leaves. I realise we have nowhere to go. Maybe she is saving it for when we go back home. I panic at the thought. I cannot go back. I stare down into the woman's hands. I cannot look into the distance and see it again. She pulls out a handful of sheikals. I haven't seen that many sheikals in a while. My stomach rumbles as I think of how much food those sheikals can buy us. Mama will be happy. I will bring money for food. The woman takes it and walks off. I have a handful of sheikals. I run upstairs. 'Mama, mama, look, look what I have.'

She wakes up, startled, and grabs my hand. 'Where did you get that from, Fatima?'

'I sold the dress.'

She sits up sharply and takes the money from me. Her lips move slightly as she counts it. She starts to cry.

'Sorry, have I done something wrong?'

'No, no, it's just it is nothing for what the dress is worth. But this is what we have now, and it will buy us food.'

The days pass and the dresses or purses or whatever else we create are sold for pittance to travellers passing by. We cannot be sure they know that each single stitch is made by hand. But we sell them. That first flutter of excitement disappears, as I realise the money does not provide much for the nights of toil that leave my mama's fingers sore and cracked from the needlework. I think of my sister. She was wearing her engagement *thobe*. I wonder how much they would pay to take the clothes off our backs, clothes they look at like costumes. But we smile and pass them over with sore fingers and the travellers pass by with a souvenir from their trip. We have no choice. Sheikals buy food, which is more necessary than our pride.

Mama becomes lost in the blood-red stitches as she retells our stories in our clothes. We wear them on our bodies. We can afford to keep the cheaper ones in the fabric we get from others. We make them fit, then we embroider them. The fabric isn't the best quality; it scratches my skin, unlike the ones Baba used to buy us before. But we get used to them. Our skin toughens underneath. And in a way, it doesn't matter. It is the style, the cut, the stitching, that is important. It shows us who we are and where we come from. She stitches almond trees, palm trees, zig-zags and birds of paradise. There are four of the birds of paradise. They are together, surrounded by flowers, looking at each other, their beaks connected. My mama's birds are always connected and stitched closely together. On her dresses, in our wall hangings and in her maps of Deir Yassin, the birds of paradise adorn the corners. And so, I follow. The days begin to take on a structure of life in the Old City, of prayers together and the desperate need to find food. Every single day. And it is like this that we continue.

After some time, we start to build a community again; a community in need of being together, of helping one another. Our doors and food cupboards, our rooms, are open to share with others who arrive with nothing but trauma on their backs. We work to build something together. We spend late nights in circles together, away from the windows, and in candlelight, we create new stitches. These stitches are keys of our old homes, of the Palestinian flag, of barbed wire that creeps around the villages that are ransacked. We extend dresses to the refugees that turn up here month after month, as the same thing that happened to us is repeated throughout the country. We add on pieces of fabric from flour sacks and whatever we can get hold of.

Every time the day it happened to us sneaks into my mind, I close my memory to it. I do it over and over again until I stop seeing my sister. Until I forget what Baba looked like, what Mohammad's laugh sounded like and the games Ibrahim and I used to play together. Whenever I hear them call my name, I pretend I don't hear them. When I see someone their age walking through the streets I turn and run in the other direction. When people call 'Yassini' I ignore them. I will forget for just as long as I have to, so I won't hurt anymore. I will forget their faces for just as long as it takes for the pain to go away and then when it has, I will remember them again. I will see them, and I will see them as they were before, not how they were on that last day. Not on that last day. Not on that last day. They are not there. They are not there lying in the field, face down in their own blood. They are not there under the earth. He is not there in the quarry. He was not taken back to the quarry. She is still in the streets of Jerusalem. She is a teacher now just as she dreamt she would be. She has returned now, and she is an even older lady than I am, but she is still more beautiful, and she is still kinder than me. We are stuck here but they are not. They are free and they are as Mama stitched them. They are birds of paradise soaring above the stone city, they are not trapped inside its walls. After all these decades of forgetting, I know now everyone I see is different to how they used to be. I see them as stitches of gold thread against blackness. They are constructed in my dreams through their voices and how they made me feel next to them, as part of them.

They are together just as I will be with them. They are in paradise, in our gardens of figs and almonds and palaces built of gold.

Gold lasts longer than stone.

I want to live with them in their palaces of gold. I want to see Lulu's face and I want her to see mine. So, I must join the land of the living and prepare myself. I have my own story to tell of that day.

I hear Suhair arrive; she is busying herself with the preparations of what is to come. They will arrive soon and once they do, they will bring her with them. I wonder what she knows. I wonder who she looks like. I wonder if she looks like her.

I sit in my favourite chair. It isn't mine. It was my husband's. My walking stick is next to me. I iron out my mama's *thobe* with my hands. I can feel the birds of paradise underneath my fingertips. I remember my mother briefly. She is holding me before it happened. The time she was happy, before. I take a deep breath and remind myself. I will tell them of the village, of its beauty and abundance. I will tell them that it was the closest thing to heaven on this earth. I will tell them how we used to dance and sing and dream of our future. I will tell them some of what happened that day. The other part is mine.

But first, she will come.

Layla.

Chapter 4

THE CAMERAS AND FILMING equipment are set up in the first room of the house.

'We are ready for you.'

I walk into the lounge, the one room in the home that is used for guests and has their best sofa, curtains and table in it. I am seated next to my aunt and uncle who are adjusting their microphone wires. Some papers are placed face down on the table. A pitcher of mint and lemon water sits on the dressed table. I pour it out for us all and begin.

I start by telling my uncle that I had found what I believed to be Tata's *thobe* and inside it was a document mentioning our family name and the village, Deir Yassin. I ask what he knows about it. My voice doesn't sound like me. I feel guilty that Tata isn't here anymore and that I am not on this trip with my dad. Her space in the house, in the family, left a gaping hole, a generational gap. Another life and everything she had been through, gone. In a way, that is why I agree and continue to film despite feeling nauseous since my arrival. It is my life's work, and although it hasn't been a long one yet, it feels consuming. There are many days and years that I have spent sitting at a keyboard writing and writing, wondering who I was writing for, who would even read it, and if it would even make the tiniest bit of difference. But I felt like I had to try. I have to try and make a difference, even if it feels like a tiny flutter in a violent storm, I have to try. And with that thought, we begin as the cameras roll.

'Your dad didn't tell you because he found it hard to know how to.'

'Tell me what?'

'Your Tata was not originally from Jericho...'

'But this is her house, her childhood home. She has lived here all her life and now you all live here.'

'She moved here when she was married,' my uncle says.

'So, she is not from here?' I know what is coming next, but I feel sick, and I don't want him to say it. I don't want everything I believe about this beautiful life to be shattered around me.

'She was born in Deir Yassin.'

My uncle turns the document over. It is my Tata's birth certificate. I can read the small bit of ink that mentions her place of birth, Deir Yassin. It is in Arabic, but I know enough to read out the letters. They match the paper sewn into her *thobe*. She was a daughter of Yassin.

'Why did no one tell me?'

'It isn't something we speak of much. Because of what happened there,' he stops short, glances at the director behind the camera, and continues. 'But we loved Yassini people so much. I chose my wife from there.'

My aunty is next to him.

'You are from Deir Yassin too, Aunty?'

'Yes, my family was from there.'

Everyone I loved was linked to this place and all of them now lived, scattered.

All this time I had searched for her roots in Jericho. In the *tatreez* of her dress, in the cut of the gowns, in the meals that were served and in the stories that were told but I had never known of Deir Yassin as her childhood home. Suddenly, her smile seems even more poignant. How does anyone move on from that? I don't know how I ever could after witnessing such horror.

'They had to leave everything behind. Our gold is buried there. Our belongings, our money, our livelihoods.'

'Why don't you go and get it back?'

'We aren't allowed to go back. None of us are allowed to go there.'

The cameras continue to roll but the director addresses me.

'I know you must have a lot of questions, but we will go to Deir Yassin. If you want to tell the family and the viewers that is where we will go next, then first thing tomorrow, you will go and meet a historian there. He will tell you about that day.'

My first thought is that I don't want to go. Why would I? I didn't even know it still existed.

'Wait, you can go to Deir Yassin?' I ask.

'Yes, the grounds are there. We can access half of them. There is a psychiatric hospital on the grounds that is fenced off, but we can go there.'

Every part of me wants to avoid it but this is what I came for. To know the truth. We must finish and he isn't allowed to tell me anymore. We have to move on to the next location and it needs to be revealed on camera. I am so distracted that

I know my next lines sound just as contrived as my first ones on arriving here.

'I will go there for you.'

I am supposed to say that. It leads nicely to the first discovery I have made. That Tata was born in Deir Yassin, miles from Jericho, closer to the Old City than here. My grandfather owned land and houses in Jerusalem. My dad had tried to tell me before; he had just never finished.

I am allowed to go to Deir Yassin because I have a British passport and, on this trip, I haven't been restricted to the West Bank only.

The crew start putting the cameras away. We take off our microphones and almost on cue, more family arrive through the open door. There are greetings and warm welcomes and my uncle has brought trays of food. My aunty is swift in turning the living room into an impromptu dining hall. Chairs are assembled around a plastic table that has been brought inside from the garden. The trays of food hold falafels, hummus, fresh breads, pastries and salads. Cold drinks are brought in from the fridge and laid out on the table. The crew come and sit with my uncles as everyone chats and eats. I don't eat because I still can't keep anything down. I have work to do first. I look around at everyone and wonder how we have been brought together, in a house full of life in this very moment. My cousin, Sumaya, is telling them she wants to get into media; she is a natural with them all. Amira brings in a bag of personalised keyrings with a poem about our family and Palestine. She gives them to everyone in the crew. It makes my heart full, their generosity and kindness. Amongst it all, we dig around and in these rare moments, we find light.

***

In the morning, I am ready. I know today is Deir Yassin. The anxiety, the nerves, everything has been building to this day. At breakfast, I still can't eat. The director comes over and sits on the chair opposite me. 'Today is going to be a tough day. But I know with the family you have, you will get through it.'

I am not sick this morning. The lack of food is helping me survive even though my stomach still burns as we approach the crew van. It is a new experience for me. I try to accept that and take stock of it all. An easy-going crew, on location. An award-winning director directing a story with our family in it. A professional crew. The setting will transport anyone who watches. I don't know what it will be like pieced together but the scenery they have shot is stunning. It helps me to focus on the practical side of it. An ice box full of snacks and drinks, the cameraman checking equipment, and the sound guy checking batteries and wires. I am the only one who isn't working. It takes the focus off me so I can cope with it. They ask if I will write any more novels. I say, never again. I know that isn't true.

The drive from Jerusalem to Deir Yassin is a short one. It is positioned high on a hilltop. The entrance is an opening in a gated fence. In front, new signs show a recently built psy-chiatric hospital. A green sharp pointed fence barricades the hospital grounds in. Surrounding it, there is a road that circles from the entrance to the exit. A park where Israeli children are playing basketball. There are two Jewish schools, with pupils running and playing on the grounds. I expected it to be dere-lict, but its normalcy throws me off. April 9, 1948. Do people know what happened here? The voices of children hang in the air. I am in the van, waiting. I am not ready to go outside. Instead, I take in the scene around me. In front of the schools, I see a man sitting on a bench. He is leafing through piles of paperwork. The crew is there, getting him set up. I wonder who he is. What he will tell me. When his microphone is set up, I am waved over. The feeling of dread is back. What is he going to tell me? I pretend I don't see the wave. The director jogs over to the van. 'You are going to meet a historian. He knows about your family. Are you ready?'

I nod my head, unable to say yes because I will never be ready. But it is historical. I am separated from that day by a generation, a lifetime. It is history. It is the past. This isn't my fault. I step out of the van onto the soil of Deir Yassin. The psychiatric hospital in the distance behind metal green gates looks like an odd site, towering in the air. I think I see figures behind the gates. Shadows in the houses. Is it my imagination? My heart is beating fast.

'*Salam*,' he greets me gently and places his hand against his chest. 'I am Umar,' he introduces himself. He tells me he has studied history since school, but he was never taught Palestinian history, so he began to research it himself.

I smile and nod. I try and glance at the papers he has.

'I have been researching what happened to your family. Do you know anything about their lives here?'

I shake my head. He is talking slowly. He is looking at me with concern. My skin feels pale and cold. I am wearing black and looking out into the distance. It is unfamiliar to me.

'The place where we are sitting right now, this is where your family house was.' He unfolds a land plan in front of me. Two houses are circled in red ink. 'This was their house, right here.' He points to another larger black ink square. 'This was your great-grandfather's stone-cutting plant. The quarry was here, and it was owned by your family and another family that lived here. They were neighbours of yours.'

'I didn't know that. So, they were stonemasons?'

'Yes, they were a very wealthy family. The land here was harvested and farmed, and they were known for being very rich. They were planning to build schools here too, so the children wouldn't have to walk to the neighbouring villages. It was renowned for its magnificent beauty, its produce, and its position near to Jerusalem.'

I am lost in the village that he recreates around me. The earth beneath my feet, the mounds of it rising and falling, the expanse that once was, the wealth they had. It feels close, as though seventy-five years haven't passed.

'I have spent a lot of time researching what happened here. Archives, survivor accounts, what we have discovered in the land. And what I am about to tell you is very difficult to hear. Are you ready for me to tell you?' His voice is soft and comforting but I can tell by the slight frown lines on his forehead and the way he bends forward and rests his hands on the papers, that he will tell me something I have not heard before.

I look out over the view. It is beautiful. The crew are silent. I notice the cars coming to collect the children from the Jewish school are slowing down. They are crawling past us to see what is happening. They can't hear what he is telling me on the bench. They shout things from their car windows. Still, I look at the view and listen to his voice.

'They had an agreement with the village next door. It was humiliating for them because the land was not rightfully theirs;

they were settlers. But they thought it meant it would keep the peace, so they signed it. They were neighbours before that, friends almost.'

'So, they would have come for dinner? Been friends?'

'Yes, yes, done business together and eaten together. But that day, they had permission to violate the agreement. The gangs waited until it was Friday prayers as they knew most of the men would be at the mosque. The gangs had shot an important man, a ruler in the village, over there the night before,' he says, pointing to the horizon I had been staring at. 'They knew the families would be alone because the men were also attending his funeral. They knew that. So, they stormed it early in the morning with grenades, guns and knives. You must understand that they were specifically targeting families, women, children.'

My mind is racing, the scenes the historian describes now fiercely brought to life as he speaks. I can see it in front of my eyes.

'They killed women and children? Do they know how many children died here?'

He nods his head and carries on telling me the details. I have to stop him because I am crying, and I can't take anymore. I did not expect to cry because it was so far away from me, but the tears come, and I can't comprehend anything else beyond it. I wonder if someone will bring a tissue, but no one moves. He carries on talking.

'Is there anything you want to ask me?'

'How many children were murdered?'

Little faces fill the land around us. I can't comprehend his answers.

He continues. 'There is a story about your great-great grandmother, the grandmother of your own grandmother Suad. Her name was Amena. She was the mother of Zainab.'

'So, my Tata Suad, it was about her grandmother?'

'Yes, her name was Amena. Her husband and son were shot in front of her. So, she picked up the gun and was martyred.'

'Tata Suad lost her grandmother here?'

'Yes, and Zainab lost her mother.'

'How many did we lose that day?'

'We found out that twenty-two members of your family were killed here that day.'

'Twenty-two?'

'Yes, the grandmother of your Tata Suad, her husband and their children were among those who were killed.'

I take deep breaths. I knew it was coming. That is why I felt so sick. I have no words left. So, after a few minutes of pause, he continues. My tears are back, this time silently streaming down my face. There were twenty-two scrapbooks in the trunk, that my dad kept. Twenty-two people were murdered that day in our family and my dad kept their photographs. All of them in our attic in the dark, now brought to light. This is why my dad kept them. A piece of their lives that were taken so brutally, so abruptly. Lives that were cut short among hundreds of others that day. But my Tata Suad and her mother, Zainab, survived. They escaped.

'Do you know what happened to my Tata and her mother that day?'

'I don't know. All we know, as you do, is that she escaped with her mother.' He carries on speaking. 'We have found someone who was also there that day. A survivor who saw both your family and your great-great grandmother that day. She lives in the Old City, in Jerusalem, and she has agreed to meet you. Her name is Fatima.' He unfolds the land map again. 'She lived here,' he says, pointing to the house next door to ours. 'She is the same age your grandmother, Suad, would have been today.'

'Will I get to meet her?'

'Yes, she can't wait to meet you. She was very pleased when we told her you were coming.'

She can't wait to meet me. This is a complete shock. Someone who may be the last person to see my great-great grandmother alive is here, in Jerusalem, a few miles away. I wonder what she is like. What did she see that day? Did she know my Tata Suad well when she was young? I have so many questions to ask this woman I have never met.

It is where we are going next. She is waiting for me.

I thank the historian for his dedication and his work on unearthing the secrets that they have tried to keep buried throughout Palestine. He tells me about his website, Zochrot, and how they are mapping all the old Palestinian villages and researching the truth of what happened in them. I thank him again for his work and tell him I am glad we met. He apologises for what happened to them. I tell him it isn't his fault. The director comes over and cuts us short. I ask if I can have the paperwork and the maps. I think he says yes. The director asks me to walk with him away from the bench. When I turn around, Umar is leaving but there is more I want to ask him. It is as though I want to recreate it in more detail. There are still so many unanswered questions. But the director is moving along with the crew; they need to film me in Deir Yassin after I have just found out. He wants my initial raw reaction to what I have just heard.

'Are you angry?'

'I don't feel angry. I feel disappointed.'

I am trying to process it, but I keep tearing up when I think of how a mother can lose a child that way. I can't remember what I say or how the words come out. I am angry as well. I don't know exactly how to feel. What I see is the children. They could be ours. It is no different that they do not belong to us. Then it sinks in. They do belong to me. There are twenty-two people and a hundred and fifty more that are no longer alive, and countless more in other villages around Palestine that are not here.

I look through the green fences at the houses inside. They are built with limestone from the quarry at Deir Yassin.

It is hard for me to tell you everything. This is the only way I can process it.

It was a quiet Friday morning on April 9 1948 a man had been shot in the village near the horizon we were looking towards the men had left to go to Friday prayers at Al-Aqsa Mosque leaving the women children and elderly behind they were stormed by Jewish gangs who stormed the village with knives, grenades and guns blood screaming your great grandmother lived here your Tata would have been a child the massacred people in plain sight they keep telling me about the pregnant women whose babies they delivered with a knife I can't stop thinking about it most of those that were slaughtered that day were women children and the elderly blood screaming those that survived were paraded around the villages in trucks orphans abandoned in the Old City of Jerusalem others brought back to the quarry and shot the quarry that builds the city that built their wealth and gave them their livelihoods they keep telling me about the blind man who said I am infirm there is no need to kill me and they laughed and killed him with a blade they shot them in the quarry the limestone covered in blood it was part of their plan one so brutal that it made other Palestinians flee one plotted despite their agreement of peace blood screaming they shot them in the quarry there were many villages like this there are many villages where this happens it is still happening they keep telling me about that they made their children kill a sibling to save their own lives I can't stop thinking about it April 9 1948 everything was left behind but they thought they might return just like those other Palestinians believed they would return they have their keys to their houses they have their gold buried in the gardens they have their clothes in the wardrobes their children in the ground in their arms in the ground on the ground it could have been my children our children us left behind on a quiet Friday morning when they knew the men would be at Friday prayers and they knew the women and children would be alone they left them safe in their stone houses built with their own two hands they hid under the dead animals under the barn that's how they survived it could have been my children or your children or anyone's children left behind they were making dinner they were playing in the gardens but when they arrived back it was too late twenty-two people in your family died that day ever since the day has echoed and reverberated around history denied denied denied despite and yet the survivors tell their story they keep telling me your great great grandmother picked up a gun and was the first one martyred after her son and husband were shot and I can't stop thinking about that she picked up a gun and was killed trying to save her family your Tata her daughter survived and we tell their stories and we won't forget April 9 1948 what you left behind on a ground that is underneath our feet as you dance on top of it.

Girl.

Part 1

WE LIVED IN A house that was full. Full of love, full of us. But as I grew older, I wanted to find myself and I wanted to do this through the way we are all taught, through career, educational attainment, money, and owning a home. I would 'make it' by having all the things you are supposed to have in life. I set my 18-year-old sights on it. I would eventually 'be' someone.

The boat cut across the water. We left the hotel rooms behind us and went to a place across the Wharf. The gleaming towers dominated the cleanly swept streets. I peered through the closed elevator doors. This was it. This was HQ. It seemed a world away from the small farming branch that I had worked in previously. It was the world I wanted to be a part of. And so, I said out loud, I am going to work here. I am going to work my way up to a place in HQ. I knew the people who worked here, in their smart tailored suits, clicking away on Blackberrys, riding home on the Tube late after a day making important decisions. It was the job I wanted, to be someone who had that life.

It took a few years of exams, long hours and hard work to climb the banking hierarchy. Eventually, I made it to the Wharf. The days passed with long hours, meetings, and after-work dinners. The evenings were filled with more studying for my finance exams. It was a normal day when one of the teams from HQ came down to visit me in the branches. We are looking for someone to work in Head Office. It was here. My ticket to the tower.

As I write, I can vividly remember the view of the water below, the city above and the towers in the distance. This is the view I had dreamed of.

The days weren't easy. I often felt out of my comfort zone. Months passed and the feeling of newness wore off. The daily grind took over. I was working on a pilot project that meant most of the advisors I worked with would be out of jobs in a few years. It didn't feel right; the goals were not aligned with mine. The work ethic was all-consuming, as though nothing existed outside of the glass tower. The pace was relentless. Every aspect of it was inflated in its importance. Everything in me was expected to be fully bought into their vision. There is so much I can say, but it is not for now. The important part of it was that as time passed, it felt as if it was nothing I wanted to be a part of. What was wrong with me? It had taken years to get here. I had everything I wanted, didn't I?

I remember sitting in the apartment I owned, waiting to leave for work, unsure why this feeling had started to pervade my thoughts. The apartment, a tiny one-bedroom set inside a huge Victorian mansion cut up into flats, had become claus-trophobic. Its exterior held the grandeur of its early days and it was a solid building, but inside, I couldn't breathe. And I was trapped into paying for it.

I left to catch the 6.08am train. This was repeated day in, day out, with only some respite at the weekends. I would spend them going out, shopping for beautiful clothes and shoes, or having groups of friends over (who were more acquaintances than friends). For a time, it had been a good distraction. But now, it was shifting. I don't know where the idea had come from, or if like all thoughts it had slowly been sewn into my mind over time through conversations one hears; the idea that being in the rat race wasn't the only type of existence to be had. There was another one. I had started to realise that I needed the other one.

This weekend was to be different as my dad was visiting. The visit was fairly relaxed but not one I was fully ready for or expecting. And yet, despite this and the general distance between us, I told him how I felt. Like I had everything, but it felt like nothing. He answered gently. 'Every person has a soul, even these birds you have,' he said, pointing to my pet cockatoos that were pecking around the corners of my rug, free in my living room, as I hated seeing them caged in. 'Even they have souls inside them. There are some things that this life can give you, but only certain things satisfy your soul. Why don't you travel and see us? Take some time out from London?'

Ideas began forming in my mind. There are places where people go to find themselves. That's where I wanted to go. Halfway around the world where life was different to the London commute from my small flat. It was the ultimate escape. I could have dismissed it as a pipe dream but the more I thought about it, the more it took over. It would be my answer to everything. Maybe that was the reason I never fitted in here? Because this wasn't the right place for me? I wouldn't have to work at the bank anymore. I could quit my job. I could leave the stress and expectations behind. If I quit my job and stayed in England, that would mean I would have to go home, and I had only been away for three years. It hadn't been long enough. I would return with everyone saying it hadn't worked. It had – I was successful – but I just didn't want it anymore, it didn't feel important to me. If I went further away, I could be free from everyone's expectations and wonderings. Those who travel that far away don't stay in touch. Their lives are imagined by others as we imagine travellers; far-flung places, no schedule, living a simple, pared-back life, reconnecting with themselves and the world. That was it. I had my plan. I was going to save up, get rid of my mortgage and my old life and be free, miles and miles away from everything I knew.

I began to search for places to travel to. The destination I landed on was Southeast Asia. I would start with Thailand. Why? It was miles away from London and the images of it were paradise! I bought postcards for my desk at work. The images of beaches and wooden-painted boats on the shoreline were pinned to my noticeboard. I bought travel guides to Thailand and learnt about the places I wanted to visit and the ones I didn't mind missing. I even looked further afield. After Thailand, where to next? I read how long a few thousand pounds could last in Southeast Asia – a couple of years, the guidebooks said. I wondered how long I would last. I would take as long as I needed to find it.

I no longer shopped for clothes; instead, I found myself in the shops specialising in outdoor clothing, spending hours wondering if I would need lightweight towels and mosquito nets. Definitely a cagoule, because of the monsoons. This time when I looked out the window at work, the river morphed into a grey snake and the rain beat down relentlessly against the glass windows and the tower's grey frame. I was going to get out of here and find whatever it was I was looking for.

Fatima.

Chapter 5

IT IS THE EVENING of Lulu's engagement. In a few months, she is due to be married. We have invited the neighbours for dinner too, to celebrate. I am busy helping my mother lay the table. It is a large gathering, so we have placed the two tables together outside in the back garden, overlooking the city below us. It is a warm night, and we sit down under the stars. The almond trees are blossoming, and the delicate pale pink and white petals float down like spring snowflakes.

Baba gives Lulu her gift. It is a beautiful solid gold bangle. It is heavy and embossed with zig-zag patterns intertwined with the moon.

'Oh baba, it is too much!'

'You are a young woman now, my beautiful girl. And so even as you grow, I want you to remember how much we all love you and are proud of you. I am sure you will be just as good a mama as your mama is.'

There are soft whispers from our guests, commenting on the generous gift, on the blessings bestowed on the family they have joined.

'Baba, I am not leaving yet. We still have so much time together.'

She slips the bangle onto her dainty wrist. It looks heavy and shines with the newness of polished gold. 'I promise I will take good care of it. Thank you both so much.'

I watch her. It is like I am in front of her now, around the same table. I can smell the food; I can see them all. My brothers are there, scooping out yoghurt and tearing the chicken for me because they think I am a baby and I might choke on the bones.

I watch Lulu. She has everything, and now this. I don't think it's fair. I slip away from the table and go to our bedroom. I can still hear them talking and laughing as their voices are carried through the nighttime air. Lulu comes to find me. She sits on the bed and strokes my hair. I want to just dwell on that moment before I move on. I want to see her again in that moment. The one I have after has ruined me. I want to see her then. She was wearing her new *thobe*. The one she and Mama had made together, especially for this night. I reach out and touch it. It is cream with rich, red stitches.

Her dark honey-coloured hair falls to her waist. She twists it around her fingers as she does when she is talking to me, 'Come on, little sister. Don't sit in here all by yourself, come back to the garden with me.' I don't want to speak to her. So, I don't answer. I find myself looking at her bracelet.

'Ah, you are upset because of my bracelet? You know, Baba is fair. He will buy you one too when you are older.'

I am frowning, my lips are stuck together, and I can't find any words to speak to her.

'Okay, well, how about you wear this for me?'

I sit up.

'Go on, put it on.' She slips it over my hand and onto my wrist. 'There, that looks beautiful on you. Will you take care of it for me?'

I nod my head. She kisses me on the forehead and leaves me behind. The revelry outside continues and just as I am about to join them, I hear my name.

'She is just a child. She will grow up soon enough.'

I can't make out exactly what they are saying but I know they are laughing at me. I storm out of the bedroom and away from the house, leaving them all behind.

I sit under my favourite tree, sobbing. Suad finds me. She is trying to tell me that everything will be okay, but I am too angry to listen.

'Take this,' I say. She refuses. 'Take it just for tonight. I don't want to wear it and I am not giving it her back!'

'No, Fatima. I can't.'

'Take it, or I will bury it right here,' I say, scraping the soil back with my fingers.

'Fine, give it to me or you will lose it. But I am bringing it back tomorrow whether you like it or not,' Suad says, slipping the bracelet onto her wrist and hiding it under the long sleeves on her *thobe*. I watch her run off in the dark. I dust off the soil and fall asleep under the tree.

***

I wake up with the sun already risen in the sky. I don't know what time it is, but it is well past dawn. It is Friday and the men will go to the prayers. Have they left already? I feel my wrist. It is bare. The bracelet! I need to find Suad. I can't go home without it. I see a figure walking towards me from the direction of the house. She is wearing a linen dress, covered in red stitches. Her hair flows behind her. Her feet are bare on the ground. I run in the opposite direction. I don't want her to find out that I haven't got it.

'Come back, Fatima,' I hear her call after me. She is running too, her feet moving swiftly over the ground. She catches up with me just past the almond tree.

'Where is it? What have you done with it?' she says, lifting up my sleeves to reveal my naked wrists.

I try and tell her, but she is upset with me now. 'Please, sister. Baba is going to be upset with me as well as you when he gets back. I promised him I would take care of it.'

'Has he left? What time is it?'

'Yes, yes, he has. You don't have long until they are all home. They aren't going to be happy.'

'I don't have it.' I try to explain to her, but she is rifling through my pockets and searching me as though I have hidden it somewhere. She grabs my hands and turns them over.

'Why is there soil all over your hands and underneath your fingers?' Her face looks worried. She turns my hands over again and rubs my skin with her gentle fingertips. 'Have you buried it?' She glances around and towards where I had run from. 'You have? You have buried it. Why would you do that?' she says frantically.

She runs off to where I had fallen asleep. I watch her but I am unable to speak. Something is happening at the bottom of the hilltop. She hasn't seen them yet. I can't make out what I am seeing. There are figures and groups of people. They are running through the village and throwing things into houses. Loud bangs ring out into the sky. The birds scatter. I try to swallow but my mouth is dry. I feel something rising through my body; it makes my feet unable to move as though they have been pinned to the spot. I need to shout to call my sister. She is running towards them, to the almond trees. She turns around when she hears the bang. She is far away from me now. A figure in the distance. I can see her face but not clearly. She doesn't look at me. She is on her knees in the soil. I wonder if she can see the panic in my face.

Lulu, I want to shout and scream but I cannot comprehend what I am seeing. 'Lulu,' the last time I try, there is sound. A high-pitched scream. She turns and looks at me. Her hands are covered in mud that is now covering the bottom of her dress.

'I will bring your bracelet back. It isn't there. I promise I will bring it for you, please just come here!'

She looks at me and then sees what is happening.

'RUN!'

She stumbles up, grabbing the fabric at her hem. She has slept in her *thobe* from the celebration the night before. She lifts it above her ankles and begins to run towards me, but she is too far away. She is too close to them. They are coming behind her. She stumbles and trips. Her face hits the ground. They are right behind us now. I have to run. I turn around and I don't look back. I run away from the city and the only place I think to go is towards the Old City. Towards Masjid Al-Aqsa because my baba will be there, and my brothers. I run and run as fast as I can with the air tight in my throat. I cannot think of anything else. I slip down the hillside away from home and roll in the undergrowth. It cuts up my skin. I get to my feet, and I am walking in the streets, getting closer and closer to the Old City. I look up behind me. There is smoke streaming up into the air. But I cannot hear panic this far down. I wonder why I cannot see anyone rushing to help. I look up helplessly and become disorientated in the streets. I can't stop shaking. I wonder how I am going to find all of my family. Where will they run to? Should I go back when the screams and fires stop? What shall I do? Where do I go?

Girl.

Part 2

THE ARRIVAL IN BANGKOK was an assault on the senses.
The trains pulled into the station, the main hub in the
capital, the lines and platform layered with grime and wet from
the humidity. It was an open station so when I disembarked
from the carriage, I could see the congested traffic and roads
with mopeds fanning out ahead of the traffic, weaving through
the tuk-tuks and cars. I wasn't going to stay here. I knew many
wanted to explore and, in some ways, I could see its appeal,
with its throng of noise and traffic, its offer of life and movement and chaos and perhaps the ability to become lost in it. I,
however, had come in search of an alternative. Paradise. One
with soft sand beaches, near isolation, and a wild jungle backdrop separating me from the world. To find it, I had to travel
away from Thailand's capital and head south to the islands.

There are two distinct coasts in Thailand, the Andaman
and the Gulf Seas. The Andaman has limestone cliffs towering out of the turquoise waters. It was picturesque just like
the stock background wallpapers on phones and laptops of the
idyllic islands. That was what I had come for. I had planned
my itinerary out from the start. I was to catch a train from

Bangkok down to the south, embark there, stay the night, and then cross over to the islands. It was easy, the guidebooks said. They were names that were synonymous with Thailand: Phuket, Ko Phangan. The tickets were cheap and printed instantly. An overnight sleeper train, first-class. I knew first-class would be different here, but I didn't realise quite how much. The first-class cabins provided a private room, a metal bed and a metal sink. That's where the luxury ended. Cockroaches scuttled along the floor. The smell of unusual flavours lingered around the carriages. I went with the safest option; the instant noodles that were available all over the country and here on the train. I didn't fancy the dark meat and sticky rice with its pungent smell filling my carriageway. I began to feel nauseous, but that soon dissipated as soon as the train pulled away from Bangkok station.

After a short while the window view changed from the choked-up city to rice paddies and intermittent rainforest trees. It soothed me. It was so vastly different from the landscapes I had seen before in my life, the most recent in the British countryside, with its tame rolling green fields of flat grass or delicate ears of wheat and harvests blowing in the breeze. Or the grey London skyline. The sharp temperament of seasons, from bitter cold snow and icy rain to long hazy summers. Here the air was heavy and wet, the skies cloudless and blue, changing instantly into monsoon rainfalls of the largest raindrops I had ever seen. I had always loved the rain, but like everything here, it felt alien, detached from the world I thought I knew. I realised how little of it I had seen. How little I had travelled. And yet it consumed me. Nothing I had considered would make me happy actually did. I worked for years to climb the corporate ladder for the job of my dreams, to get to the place I had always imagined working in. I had everything that was supposed to make you happy: beautiful things, my own apartment, a job my friends were all envious of. And yet I couldn't express to anyone how I felt inside. Like the closer I got to having everything, the more it felt like nothing. And of course, I knew why. Because we are supposed to be free, aren't we? To travel, to explore.

I must admit I felt the pressure and stress leave me the moment I finished my notice. The moment my phone wasn't set with alarms for waking up, alarms for the train timetable, alarms for meetings, one after another. Suddenly time didn't matter. What day of the week it was didn't matter; it was all about the present. The moment. My life was just what was in my backpack. The best-branded rainmacs, mosquito nets and blow-up sleeping equipment. Flares, an emergency medical kit and a few changes of clothes. Even the relinquishing of my belongings felt freeing. I no longer needed work suits, make-up, a dozen shoes. Just a pair of travelling sandals and my shirt dress. The ultimate freedom. I could go wherever I wanted with the bag on my back and cash in my purse.

I had even left my mobile phone behind. I was absolutely sure I didn't mean to but when I boarded the plane, I didn't have it. I didn't panic. I was relieved, which made me think... did I accidentally leave it behind or had I subconsciously done it so I couldn't be contacted for a while? I am not sure I have ever worked out the answer to that.

The thought took me back home, to our family house. My mum's tears as I left. Her fears of the danger of me travelling around Asia, so far from home. So alone. London was bad enough for her. I remembered a phone call just before 9pm one evening, 'Why aren't you home yet? You can't be out alone in the city at this time. Call me as soon as you get back.' I looked around the packed carriage, people still piling on and off tubes as they met friends for dinner or headed out with colleagues. But this. I told her how safe it was, and how many travellers did it, and in all my excitement and trepidation, I never gave it a second thought. As if every problem in my life would be solved if I just managed to save enough money and go far away to the tropics, to the places where people go to find themselves, to find their life purpose.

I pulled out my notebook. It was the one thing I needed to start over. I had read once that if you are resetting your life, you need to know what it is you want. Many of us don't know anymore, so a therapist recommended writing about what you used to love. Get a blank sheet of paper and write down everything you have ever said you wanted to do or be when you grew up. I wanted to be a vet, so I wrote that down. I wanted to travel, so I wrote that down. I wanted to help people.

I remembered my school days. My favourite subject was English, especially creative writing. I loved to write stories. My mum said she often wondered where I was during the daytime, only to discover I was in my room, reading. I could recite the whole Beatrix Potter collection almost by heart by the time I was twelve. I read ghost stories, mysteries and classics. I loved, more than anything, to write and tell stories. I would tell my sister stories in makeshift tents in our bedrooms, or scary stories when we camped out in the garden at night. My imagination turned everything around me into a world of possibilities and wonders. I imagined our neighbours were witches, stalking us in the night, after watching Roald Dahl. I imagined them trying to snatch us from my dad's apartment, where we stayed at the weekends, as we played amongst huge trees in wooded gardens. Stories gave the world a new depth that I could immerse myself in.

My A-Level grades were high. I had always excelled academically so applying for an English Literature degree seemed a natural choice. But I stalled. University was expensive. I didn't want a pile of debt. My career advisor told me I should go. I could be a teacher or a journalist. So, I did work experience at my local newspaper. You had to be brash to get the story and ask people uncomfortable questions. The newspaper rooms were noisy, and the printing of the papers was so loud you had to wear headphones. I remember the journalists' chaotic desks, round-the-clock hours and bravery in asking questions nobody else wanted to. I remember leaving realising that it wasn't for me. I was disappointed. I didn't want to be a teacher; I had spent enough time in school. I didn't want to be a journalist; I wasn't confrontational enough. I couldn't make people feel uncomfortable without feeling that way myself. I was stuck. What was I going to do? What I loved in terms of career was not going to offer me what I needed to live a comfortable life. So, I chose finance.

The view became darker and darker as night fell. I looked at my watch. Over nine hours left. Eventually, I was lulled to sleep by the promise of where I would be when I opened my eyes.

After around twelve hours, the train pulled into the final station. We had been carried through the night down to Thailand's southern coast, Surat Thani. I stepped off the train, relieved to be in the fresh dawn air of a new city, but I had no plans to stop in the city. I pulled out the foldable map that I had marked eagerly back in the office during lunch hours. I would go into the empty grey conference rooms and lay it out on the glass-topped tables, marking each part of my journey. I looked down at the pen markings. I looked around. The landscape was so noticeably different to London that it made my heart skip. I had made it. I had finally done what many dream of. The realisation pulsed through my body and gave me a vigour I hadn't felt for a long time. I was almost at my destination.

I left the station and headed towards the exit. It was full of taxis and tuk-tuk drivers, shouting prices and names of islands that they could drive us to. I heard the name Ko Phangan. That was it. The larger and more famous of the two islands, Ko Samui, was the usual destination for travellers and tourists. But its neighbour, Ko Phangan, was quieter and more scenic, famous for its full moon parties. Less touristy, I had read. I bartered for a tuk-tuk and combined bus ticket price I didn't mind paying, and joined a few others on the ride through the city to a bus station. The bus wasn't due to arrive for an hour or so, so I waited by a river alongside others I assumed were tourists (we weren't a hard crowd to spot, decked out in travel gear, backpacks strapped onto our backs). I sat watching the water swell and rise. It was dark, insipid green. The rivers you imagined exist in jungles, with a colour and depth that only belonged there. I watched the water, lulled by nature after days of travelling through airports and train stations, hordes of people, in and out, to and fro, all trying to reach their destination. I was so far from my old life that I was finally beginning to breathe.

Layla.
Chapter 5

THE SUN SINKS INTO the horizon over Deir Yassin as we speak. I didn't think I would feel as emotional as I do, because the event was historic, a part of the past. I thought it happening so long ago meant I would be detached from it. But that isn't reality. Time does not heal all. To be human is to feel, and this is all I can do. It is the least I can do.

We drive to Jerusalem the following morning. We park up on a side street and walk through the Old City streets. I can't help reaching out and touching the stone that built the walls and homes. It is Yassini stone. We reach a cave-like entryway in the streets. I wait in the cool shade of the tunnel as the camera crew set up. They have met her before, but I haven't. I am nervous to meet her. I have the opportunity to talk to her about Deir Yassin, but I am acutely aware that she may not want to live through it again, just as my own Tata did not. At least not to me. And who am I but a stranger, one that half belongs to a foreign land, and to add to it, the land that abandoned Palestine in 1948. Now I am here, in her home, asking her to remember a day that no one should ever have had to live through, let alone relive.

I turn to the entrance and see two children, young, maybe two and five years old, hand in hand, walking down the stone steps in the city as the *athan* sounds from Al-Aqsa. I wonder what it is like to grow up in the Old City with Masjid Al-Aqsa as their main mosque. What a childhood it is, where they can walk barefoot through the ancient streets and call it home.

'She is ready for you.'

Fatima.

Chapter 6

MY SONS ARE BUSY preparing coffee for our guests. I hear them arrive. She is waiting in the entrance. She is waiting to meet me just as I am waiting to meet her. They ask me to walk to the door. My heart is pounding because I do not know who I will see this morning, but I know she is a part of me in a way she could never imagine. I take my stick and walk the short distance to the doorway. She is walking up the steps. I cannot hold it in any longer. I grab her and lift her from her feet and kiss her cheeks. My dear Suad, it is as if it could have been her standing at my door. After all this time. She is here.

We sit down together in the living room, hand in hand. I watch her thanking me and with each movement of her mouth, I imagine it is Suad. I am talking to her, asking her where the treasure is buried, if she can remember. But she smiles at me and looks towards Amir. I forget she can't speak Arabic well. Amir is her translator; I was there when his mother was born. He is from a good family. I agreed for him to translate because I have to trust who is telling my story, the words that come out of my mouth. He is busy setting up. They will begin recording soon so I switch away from my present and I return to the day. I will ask her later.

'I don't even think I said, I am Layla,' she says. Layla. Does she know something? My brain is agile. It remembers the minutest detail. Her name is Layla.

'Did you know my grandmother? Suad?' Layla asks me.

She seems to have no idea how much she looks like Suad. I remember her when I look at her. She is so like her, it takes me a while to see anyone else but my old friend.

'Yes, we were the closest of friends, Suad and I. We did everything together. We rolled vine leaves with our mothers, we stitched together, we shared dinners together, we spent every day together.' My mind drifts off as Amir translates it to her. I see Suad in the fields smiling, and then I see her again. The image snaps back to the orphanage. She barely recognises me. I never saw her again after that day. My eyes start to cry silently. All this time.

'So, we are neighbours,' Layla says, holding my hand.

'No, we are family. She was my sister, and you are mine.'

'That means so much to me, to meet you and for you to welcome me as family.'

'You are my family, they were my family.'

I have brought up the past. I see Layla's eyes move uncomfortably to the floor. She wants to ask me about it. I can tell.

'What was life like before?' Layla asks.

I tell her how beautiful it was. How we used to run freely in the fields and live off its produce. How Suad's mother Zainab and grandmother Amena were full of life. How all our mothers were, before. How they danced at weddings. How Amena opened her doors and welcomed us, our neighbours, even the settlers who came that day. Before it happened, we were neighbours. I believed friends once, but I can barely say that in the same sentence now. I see them running towards us. We shared food once. I hear screaming and gunshots. I stop. I close my eyes. When I reopen them, I just see Suad in front of me. It is Layla. But to me, it is her. They all begin to fill the room around us. All the ones we have lost.

'You don't have to answer if it is too hard, but do you remember that day?'

She asks me where I was that day.

'In the gardens,' I answer. I don't say I am with my sister, but I see her now in the room with us. Does she know?

'Did you see Suad, Zainab and her mother, Amena? They lived together, didn't they?'

I nod. I am unsure what to tell her. She is young and her eyes plead with me, with hope. I have seen it before in the young.

'I saw them all. Zainab, Suad, and Amena. They were making dinner in the kitchen for when the boys arrived home from the prayers.' I left time for Amir to translate and for me to continue. 'I shouted "We have to leave, they're coming for us", but they didn't come with me. I didn't wait. I couldn't. "Run. We will follow."' I think that is what Zainab said, but I left them. Suad just followed her mother, sticking closely to her legs like a lamb that doesn't know which way to turn. Zainab abandoned preparing the meal and took Suad's hands. Suad's eyes looked back at me, confused. Not yet terrified. What I don't tell the film crew is how calm Amena was. She did not move. She kept looking out the door. She was waiting for her boys.

'Were you scared?'

There are other things I saw that day that I have never told anyone. I will not say them now. Layla repeats her question.

'Of course we were scared. It was hell on earth that day. They robbed everything from us in the most appalling, inhuman, most violent of ways. Of course I was scared.'

I see Lulu as I did that day. Her figure is in the room with us. I am reminded of why I am doing this. For her. For the promise I made her all those years ago. I can't remember what else I say. I forget where I am for a moment. I drift again. I am brought back to my living room, opposite a woman I loved in a life way before this one. She looks so much like my Suad. My eyes only see Suad. She is asking me questions. Do I know where their treasure and belongings are buried? I can't imagine how much gold is buried there. Gold and treasures of the life we left behind. I never wanted the treasure because it meant I would have to return. It is only because I am reminded of my promise that it means something to me once again. But not for the riches of this life. I turned them down years ago because I refused to sell my soul for the pittance of this world. As my eyes scan the grounds and the lands and the houses, I am back there but I know today it will be unrecognisable and even more difficult for me. I need Suad. Only she knows.

'Did you see Suad again after that day?'

I shake my head. The words didn't leave my mouth so I haven't mouthed a lie. But I cannot tell this young girl how I left her grandmother. I will not do that to her. Instead, I move to the present. 'I heard she moved to Jericho.' I am ready to ask her. 'Can I see her?'

Layla looks at the director and then back at me. She slowly shakes her head. 'I'm sorry, she passed away some time ago.'

My body is hit with a hard blow. She is gone. I thought I might get to see her again. If she is gone then the secret is buried with her. 'But you said you found Suad. Remember?' I say, this time turning to the director. Amir translates.

'Yes, Suad's granddaughter. I am sorry. I thought we told you.'

My heart races. Lulu disappears out of the room. She looks sad. It would hurt less if she looked angry but she seldom became angry. My body is betraying me. My hands shake slightly and I can't stop my knee from knocking up and down. My body will not calm down. After all this build-up, the belief that the last part of my life can be resolved has evaporated into the air. I look up to my sons. They can see me from the entranceway where they have been watching. They know what I am pleading with them. Make it finish.

I tell them I don't remember anything else. But as the words leave my lips, I feel that she knows. She knows what happened then. Lulu is looking at me. I take slow, deep breaths. It is time I go back there for the last time, but this is something that I will never tell another soul.

Layla.

Chapter 6

I WALK OVER TOWARDS the doorway. It is a turn of stone steps leading to an old wooden door that now leans, hingeless, towards the sides of the opening. I walk up, looking down at my steps. I have just been told what happened to my family and I am about to meet someone that lived through it. She was there. April 9 1948. A survivor of that day, just like my Tata.

At the top of the doorway, Fatima stands, a walking stick in her hand and a beaming smile on her face. She is only slightly shorter than me, yet she lifts me off my feet and presses her cheek into mine, repeating her welcomes over and over again as though we too have been separated for years. I ask the translator, Amir, to thank her for her warm welcome and tell her how much I appreciate meeting a neighbour of ours.

'You are not my neighbour; you are my family.'

She is stroking my face and rubbing my hand, comforting me. I can't believe that there was someone who had seen my Tata that day as a young girl. And she could have been one of the last people to see my Tata Amena alive.

'You look just like her. It is like I am sitting with her today. After all these years we are back together.'

She is smiling and holding my hand, looking intently at my face, asking Allah to bless me and my family. She is a similar age to Tata, and she tells me how they used to play together in the gardens. Fatima's eyes drift off, back to a time before April 1948. I go with her. My Tata is there, and her mother, Zainab, and her mother, Amena; whole generations of my family are there. I can see them for the first time in the village. She reminisces about the beauty of it, and how it is renowned for its abundance of fruits, figs and almond trees. She tells me about how Amena and Zainab were full of life. Amena was always the first one to sing at weddings and parties; she was the soul of the place. She tells me we are sisters just like she and Suad were.

Then she tells me about that day. Amir is slow in translating it. I turn to face him as he stops talking and I can't understand what she is saying but I know it is important. But Amir is weeping. He cannot voice the horrors she speaks of, so he summarises it for us. I have no words to comfort her except, 'To Allah we belong and to Allah we return.' She says it in Arabic until it soothes her. Her tears remain but her eyes reconnect with mine. I am desperate to know what happened. The truth of that day.

'I heard a story that my Tata Amena waited for her husband and sons, and when they were shot, she picked up the gun and shot back at the gangs. Do you know anything about this?'

She smiles at me. 'I don't know about that, but I know she was a wonderful mother and would do anything for her family, so it doesn't surprise me. You are so like her. It is like after all these years, Allah has brought her back to me through you.'

I take a deep breath as Amir relays it to me. Fatima was one of the last people to see my Tata Amena alive. I am grateful they have found her, and I am with her now. Although she can't tell me exactly how she died, she told me how she lived. I had been so focused on finding out what happened that day, that I hadn't considered who she really was, and how she had lived her life.

My hand is on her knee, and I feel it begin to shake after I tell her we lost my Tata. Her tears start again. Another one lost. I think it is too much now. It isn't fair to burden the living with recounting the stories of the dead. Her son comes in. 'I think she has told you everything?' The TV crew pick up the cue and start to wrap it up, thanking her for her time and her generosity. While they are busy packing, she tells me, 'I wouldn't have spoken to anyone else about that day except for you.' I hold her hand and thank her.

Fatima is calmer now. She has the strength to stand up and points to a poem on the wall in Arabic. She wants me to read it, so she calls Amir and asks him to translate it into English. Tears roll down his cheeks as he reads. The poem was written by her late husband. He spent his lifetime capturing every minute detail of Deir Yassin. His poem hangs on a stone wall in the ancient Old City of Jerusalem, in a house that was their home, and in Fatima's family, but never the place they were from. Both of them were survivors of Deir Yassin and reunited in the Old City. Together, they built a long life with many to pass on their legacy. His name was Kareem.

We sit with her sons, Mohammad and Ibrahim. They tell me about their children, her grandchildren. They pull out photo albums and photographs of the family in frames around the dresser. She is showing me her granddaughter in a graduation dress and pointing at the photo. I turn to her sons; sorry, I don't understand what she is telling me. They laugh and move her thumb out of the way. It is covering the face of Barack Obama. Her granddaughter met him in America. She represented Palestine when she met him with the Palestinian *keffiyeh* around her neck. She is coming to visit next summer. We should all come together then, and I should bring my children to her. She goes to the dresser and pulls open a drawer. In it are bags of sweets, and she thrusts them into my hands. 'For the children, for the children, may Allah bless them.'

Mohammad and Ibrahim have brought a selection of dishes from around the Old City. Every dish it is famous for is now laid out on the table, ready for us. We sit and eat and talk about life after Deir Yassin. They tell me about the house their family built here that belonged to Fatima's grandfather before that. She came here that day, to her grandfather's old home.

'These stone walls,' Ibrahim says, tapping them, 'they could tell you some stories.'

'Like when I survived the tiger stalking the old city streets,' Mohammad says.

'Sorry, did you say tiger?!'

'Yes, a large tiger was stalking the streets, and I was out late with my friend's father. We were close growing up. Anyway, I fell asleep right on those very steps outside,' he said, pointing down through the kitchen to the main doorway. 'He saw the tiger right there in the alleyway. And he shouted, "Get up, Mohammad, get up!"'

'What did you do?'

'I was fast asleep and knew nothing of it. When I woke up in the morning, I had a new nickname. The protected one.'

The truth in Palestine is always far more unbelievable than anything one could make up.

For the first time here, I hear the name called in the streets, I see it in the names of businesses. They are the Yassinis. They may have lost their land like many other Palestinians, but they have not lost their identity or their rich heritage. It is passed from generation to generation inside the walls of these houses built from Yassini stone and in the people inside them. Through us.

'This house even holds the secrets of the past. Come with me,' Mohammad says, pointing to the wall behind us that is covered with a panel of fabric. He kneels and pushes the stone. 'Do you see the marks in the stone? They are carved by the stonemason. Just like our mother stitches her *tatreez* symbols, we have our own languages.' The stone moves, revealing a passageway that winds down into the darkness.

'Where does it go?'

'To the heart of the Noble Sanctuary. That is why they offer us millions of dollars for these few rooms. To try to legitimately own this part of the city, to own these bricks that were built with our great-great grandfather's hands, to own a piece of this legacy, but it is not ours to give. Only to take care of it for other generations.'

The TV crew get ready to leave. They are thanking Fatima and her sons. I don't feel like I have had enough time here. I am not ready to leave. I feel as though I belong with Fatima. She calls me *ohkti*, her sister.

The word sister reminds me... the photograph! I remember I haven't shown it to her. She is probably the only person alive who might know who it is. I fumble around in my pocket as I hear them leaving. It isn't in there! I empty my pockets inside out. Where is it? I can't believe I don't have it with me! It is over. We must stick to the itinerary and leave. I have lost my chance.

Just as I am about to walk out the door, Amir asks me to wait. Fatima is asking him to translate something. She is whispering in his ear but holding my arm tightly, linked in hers. I think I am helping her to stand, but it is the other way around.

'She would like to know if your Tata or anyone in your family ever told you about the treasure she left behind as a child?'

I am holding her arm and looking at her as my brain tries to unravel our conversations, her stories. Her treasure was rarely in gold. 'She says it is very important, she left something behind that day and your Tata knew where it was –' he pauses as she continues, trying to translate her words as quickly as she is saying them, '...buried, she thinks it could be something buried in Deir Yassin.'

'I'm sorry, Fatima, I don't know. She never mentioned it to me.' I hold her hands, desperately wanting to give her something she needs, just as she has done for me.

Fatima is tugging Amir's arm, there is an urgency to her words. The crew are down in the stone alleyway waiting for me. We don't have much time left. I wish I could stay.

'Anything at all? About where she was that day, back in 1948? Did she ever go back?'

'She couldn't have returned. Did you ever return?'

Fatima shakes her head. 'I have something I need to find. Please, if you remember anything, please tell me. You are my last chance.'

I desperately want to remember. But I couldn't think of what she meant.

'I'm so sorry. I have to go.'

She smiles at me, but the tears have already taken over. Amir talks to her in Arabic and eventually, she lets go of his arm. 'It is life to me, to my Layla. Please.'

Her English is broken but I understand its significance.

'I am sorry, Fatima. If I think of anything I will let you know.'

She reaches out her hands and grips mine. I notice that she has something between her fingers. She pushes a note into my hand, looking ahead towards the film crew to see if anyone has noticed. No one has. The exchange is only between us. What is it I can do for her that no one else can? I look back at her standing at the top of the stone steps. I know from then that this is a house I will come back to. That there is another part of me that belongs here in the Old City, surrounded by the family and friends of my Tata.

***

The last night there passes in a blur of memories and reconstructions but there is something that has overridden it all. It is the life of those around me. It is in their unwavering hope, it is in their optimism. I understand now it isn't just about that day. She is a survivor, and after that day, there was life. Many lives. Many lifetimes. There is her life, her mother's, her husband's, her children's and now their children's. It didn't all end on that day in April 1948. After that day, they built an extraordinary life out of the ruins. They are still building.

It was in the connection Amir had to his history. He was younger than me, but that passion, that understanding of his heritage and the fight to keep Palestinian history alive, is shared across generations. It reaffirmed that I was given this opportunity to share this history with others and keep it alive. There is hope and there is great strength. I begin to see the resilience and resistance in their lives, in the babies they birth, and in the houses they have rebuilt from stone that was once ours. The Yassinis own the land. I am a Yassini girl, and for the first time in my life, I understand why this home is one of the most important parts of my life. The physical home of ours may not always be there, but in some ways, this is higher than that. It is continually rebuilt in the minds and dreams of every Palestinian I have ever met.

Girl.

Part 3

THE FERRY MASTER SHOUTED out 'Ko Samui', where two-thirds of the ferry emptied. The last island, Ko Phangan, came into view as we sailed onwards, the sea changing from the black depths to the beautiful blues of the tropics. A short ride away from the ferry station was the only accommodation on the island I had booked; a wooden cabin on the beach, with a hammock tied between two palm trees outside. It was a simple cabin. It was made of thin planks of wood nailed together and lifted off the ground by four stilts that kept it away from the encroaching sea. I felt the wooden walls, they creaked beneath my fingers and moved under the pressure. It wasn't as solid as stone. A pebble-walled shower in the bathroom and a double bed with fresh white bedding, under a canopy of mosquito nets. That night I slept under it and could hear the rain battering the tin roof. The rainwater began to leak through parts of the ceiling, narrowly missing the bed. The mosquito nets draped around me were flimsy and moving slightly from the storm raging outside. My body rocked in bed, and I wondered if it was all in my head or if at any point the cabin would be swept away into the ocean. I imagined its stilts buckling under the pressure and the wild ocean dragging me into the blackness. It seemed impermanent, but wasn't everything? I grabbed my notebook and wrote through the storm, trying to capture its intensity, its description. Trying to take my mind off how tiny I was in this beachside cabin as the earth roared around me.

After a while, the clouds parted in the sky and the sun began to shine. I was relieved. In my darkest moments, I could envisage myself being washed out into the dark ocean with no one around me to even witness my demise. I shook off the melancholic feeling of my nothingness and replaced it with something more earthly. I was hungry. I went outside and climbed onto my moped that I had rented alongside the cabin, and went off to find some food. I was told the street markets were the best places to get something to eat and it wasn't far from where I was staying.

I drove past the odd stall and local houses, made of the same materials as my cabin but older and rougher. Even the peeling paint revealed layers of varying coloured paint jobs that had been stripped away by time, rain and sun. Foliage grew around them, concealing them from the roadside. The trees bent with the winds and their heavy green leaves shaded locals sat outside watching people pass by. The roads were wet, but the sun was warming me through, and I drove slowly so I could take in everything as I passed. Ahead of me, I smelt the food market before I saw the plethora of stalls selling everything from meats to fish to sweet Thai delicacies. The pungent smell of lemongrass permeated the air and the heavy smell of grease that fried the dark meats I couldn't decipher. I settled for a vegetarian Thai green curry. I couldn't eat much. I bought freshly boiled and toasted corn on the cob, loaded with chilli butter. Passers-by came to sit at my table. They looked seasoned, unlike me, with my clothes barely worn and my bag almost fresh from the shop back in England. They told me about a place on the island I had to go and see. I scribbled it down on my receipt paper. A cove, hidden away off the tourist trail. A place barely discovered, of unparalleled beauty. My postcard, The Beach images, flashed through my mind. I would find that next.

True to what the guidebook said, as that was all I had to go on, hundreds of tourists descended on the island for the full moon party at Haad Rin beach, a beautiful cove with an expansive sweep of white sand and traditional wooden Thai boats painted with colourful stripes. Behind the beaches were places to stay, and a plethora of bars and places to eat. The accommodation was mostly basic with people crashing in shared rooms. They weren't there to sleep.

When night fell, the beach was packed. Don't swim in the sea in the morning, the locals said. It is their toilet at night. The pristine beaches became littered with plastic cups, drug wrappers, and alcohol bottles. The air was filled with the scent of cheap beer and sweat. The crowds became intense, the music vibrated the sand beneath my feet. Everywhere I turned people were dancing and revelling, taking photographs of themselves at one of the most famous parties in Thailand.

I took refuge in a café on the cliffs overlooking the beach and watched as the night of chaos ensued. Lights and music blared from speakers that had sprung up in the corners of the beaches. Fuelled by cocktails of everything you can imagine, the partygoers told similar stories of escape, of finding paradise. Some had been there for months; for others, it had turned into years. Had they found what they were looking for? It seemed the longer they stayed, the more lost they became. The more they needed to slip away into another world of drugs and alcohol, to escape whatever it was they were looking for but couldn't find.

I left the island shortly after the full moon. I sought out the Andaman Islands on the west side of the islands where the limestone cliffs dominated the coastal landscape. I travelled through to Krabi, a southern province on the way to Ko Lanta. It was one of the islands off the Andaman coast. So, Krabi was the first place to go to explore the islands and the iconic cliffs that had decorated my office desk. The coastline was just as I had seen on all those picture-perfect postcards I had collected. Trees grew around sugar sand beaches, dappling them in shade whilst the seas rolled in varying shades of deep blue and green. I spent most of my days there, sitting underneath the shade of the trees, writing.

By the late afternoon of the following week, I decided to venture inland more. I was surprised to see mosques in Krabi as I drove through the province looking for somewhere to spend the night. Islam came to Thailand with the Muslim traders back in the thirteenth century, I read on the mosque wall. I felt like there was too much to explore in Krabi and something about the landscape and how it differed from the rest of Thailand intrigued me. I followed the signs to the street food markets, the best places to discover the heart of a place, and strolled through the stalls. Women wearing headscarves served Pad Thai and halal barbequed meat. They told me their descendants were from Malaysia and had settled in Thailand generations ago. I ate food with them and enjoyed the evening there with some company.

The next day, as I was waiting for the speedboat on the dock, I pointed to grey rubble piles rising out from the water. 'From the tsunami,' the tour guide said and carried on preparing for the trip. My feet were ankle-deep in the water. I cast my eyes out to the sea and still couldn't imagine what witnessing that must have been like. I heard many islanders didn't want to go back into the sea afterwards in case it happened again.

I climbed onto the boat and held on as we sailed through the cliffs that protruded out of the water and towered above us. The tour guide was explaining how they had formed from the fossilized bones of sea creatures. Their bones and sediment had been crushed and compressed over millions of years, resulting in the stone that now rose from the sea. Eroded by winds and sea salt, they had been naturally carved into the shapes that we see today, and they were slowly, yet continually, changing over time.

From there we went on to Phi Phi Leh, the island famous for its Hollywood movie shoots, from James Bond to The Beach. White sand beaches were shaped coves that wrapped like half-moons from the shore, against a jungle backdrop of see-through azure sea. It was some of the most beautiful scenery I had ever seen. Boats pulled up to and from the islands all day, whizzing through the water. We left as many others arrived. On the way back, we stopped at the caves. These were the caves where they sourced the ingredients for the popular bird's nest soup described as 'The Caviar of the East'. The tiny swiftlet bird uses its thick saliva to make nests which dries and becomes a home for its chicks. It was these very nests that were harvested and made into soup! I was shocked because I thought bird's nest soup was just dried noodles in the shape of a bird's nest. I never considered for one minute that it was an actual nest, taken from these dank caves in the middle of the sea.

Chains of people followed our routes; I could hear the echoes of the same stories told to them as we passed. It was then that I realised these islands were not the remote ones I had come in search of. They were so well known now that they never had quiet moments. Those ideals of finding sanctuary and solace were more likely to be found off the beaten track. Then I remembered the travellers I had met in the Ko Phangan food market. They had told me about a place that was cut off from most trails and existed on its own. A ripple of excitement ran through me as I decided that was where I would go next.

Before I left to find the place, I went to an internet café and emailed home to let them know I was safe. I hadn't bought another phone as I still relished the freedom of not having one for a while. I would reconnect soon but right now I didn't want to and there wasn't a great need with internet cafés all over Thailand. I wrote all about the places I'd seen so far, as I knew my mum would appreciate it. She loved to travel. Especially to warm beaches, far from home. Who didn't? Before I left the café, I wrote in my notebook. I had the inklings of a story. I wrote until nearly an hour had passed. I tucked it away and reread the directions for finding the cove. My next mission was to head off to find the cove; a slice of paradise that had so far eluded me on my travels.

The higher I climbed up the coast, the more dramatic became the view. The sheer drops down to uninhabited beaches, adorned with yellow and fuchsia flowers with the gentle sea rolling in and beckoning me towards it. Also dotted along the coastal paths were tsunami warnings. It was only a few years before my trip that a tsunami had killed hundreds of thousands of people after a major earthquake created thirty-metre high waves. 'What if there is a tsunami again?' my mum had said. What if? I thought, but what if I never do anything because of what if? I was in my twenties; I didn't have the same fear. I had learnt nothing of life or death, so it was so far from my thoughts when she asked me, I am not sure I even answered the question. Now I was here, the scenes from the news came into my head. In case of tsunami, the signs read, with arrows pointing upwards. The escape route was to climb as high as you could from the sea. I looked down at the sea. It looked so serene I wondered how anything in the world could turn so violently. Of course, I didn't know that then. Not yet.

I continued towards the directions the travellers had given me, across the coastal road and onto a track through the rainforest, following the coast until a clearing appeared up ahead. As I ventured through the muddy dirt road, the moped bounced through the tracks and weaved through the trees, almost becoming stuck in the heavy red rainforest soil. It took a lot of effort to yank the wheels out. I wasn't sure I was following the right way. The dirt track had become almost invisible, and my moped wasn't powerful enough to get through some parts, so I had to pull it alongside me. The air was heavy under the canopy of the trees. The sunlight didn't break through so the shade provided some respite, but still, my clothes stuck to me as my body sweated under the heat of the canopy. I thought I could hear monkeys in the trees above my head, screeching.

The screech pierced through my skin, and I heard a rustling in the trees. I stopped dead. Was it an animal? I looked around, barely daring to breathe. I looked up towards the canopy. It's just the wildlife, I told myself. You are in the middle of the jungle, I said out loud. But that didn't stop the images of the news stories of dead bodies discovered in the rainforest displaying vividly in my overactive imagination. Travellers who had gone missing were found weeks or even months later. Bodies left behind. I could end up like that. I told you it wasn't safe, my mum's voice echoed through my brain. I was sure I was lost. I realised no one knew where I was. I was miles from any town and from the last place I stayed. I stopped for a few moments to breathe. I looked around. It was just jungle and trees. I walked on a bit further, abandoning my moped. Still no way out. I turned and did the same thing in the other direction and was relieved when at last I found the semblance of a track. That must be it.

With no other route or plan, I dragged my moped to the drier path and rode slowly along it, praying that I would find either the road back to the city or the place that I had been told of. I was wondering now if maybe it was a joke, a prank played on gullible tourists like me, who were looking for something that probably didn't exist anymore. I thought I would have found it by now as I had covered most of the Thai coast and taken boats to its islands. But still, it wasn't fulfilling me the way I thought so maybe the story they told me wasn't real at all. I just wanted it to be, and now here I was, completely lost.

Fatima.

Chapter 7

IDIDN'T TELL YOU everything. I keep things to myself. It is part of what we do. I didn't want it to slip out when the TV crew were filming. I had to be careful not to dishonour my dearest friend. If Suad didn't tell her granddaughter what happened, that is because perhaps she didn't ever want her to know the true horror of war. So now you know most of the story, I will tell you the rest.

After it happens, I wander to the Old City to my great-grandfather's house which my baba and brothers had been working on for months prior. As I don't know anywhere else to go, I go there. It is the only other place I know. For hours I sit hiding in the stone doorway, concealed from view. A few times I consider getting up, but I can't move. My body is frozen on the stone. I can hear the streets around me erupt with panic. I can hear people screaming about what happened. The raid. The slaughter. They are going to help. I cover my ears. I wonder how long I would sit on those steps before my family found me. It is nightfall when I see a figure appear in the shaded entryway. A figure being held up by two others. I shuffle my feet down the steps and peer around to see better.

'Mama?' I say, questioning it. Unsure of the familiar shape in front of me. Almost not daring to see my mama alive.

She looks up, and with the remaining strength she has left, she limps towards me and holds me, sobbing into my hair. I suspect she thought the same.

'Where is Baba?'

She shakes her head and sobs.

'Mohammad? Ibrahim? Lulu?'

'No, *habibte*, it is just us. Just us.'

'No, that can't be right. They were at Friday prayers, they weren't there, and Lulu...'

I pause. A flash of Lulu looking up at me from the ground. I can't see past that. Just her face looking at me as they closed in around her. Lulu. If I hadn't taken her bracelet she wouldn't have been so far out in the fields. I will find her bracelet; I will get it off Suad and when I give it back to her, she will forgive me. When I find her, we will all be together again. I keep this part a secret. One I have buried until I hear Suad's name again and it opens the chambers of my brain to that day, and slowly morphs into my present. We go inside my great-grandfather's empty stone house.

'We will go back tomorrow. At least we have somewhere to stay for the night.'

'But we should be looking for them. What if they are lost or they don't know where to come and find us?'

'Shush, shush, my baby. Just sleep. Mama needs to sleep.'

She closes her eyes and curls around me on the stone floor. I vow to stay awake all night and slip out of her grasp just as soon as I can. I drift between sleep and the present. Every time I close my eyes I see my sister's *thobe*, stained with mud as if she had been buried in it like the Qadisha Valley mummies. They were buried in their best *thobes* too. Why would anyone bury their children? I begin to understand.

It is in the next morning and the following days that I start to piece together what happened. Neighbours visit with food and blankets when they see how empty the house is. Mama doesn't eat. She is determined to go back to her home. She tries to leave the city, but they won't let her go. 'It is too dangerous. They are still there, just give it more time. Come to the *masjid*. We can see who else is there. Come, let's see. We will stay with you. Just give it a bit more time.'

'But our clothes, my baby's clothes, they are in our home. My husband built those walls with his own hands. Our business is there, my life is there, my babies are there.'

'Babies?'

'Her sons and her daughter,' I hear, 'and her husband.' All of them.

'May Allah protect us from this evil.'

But the evil stays with me. It follows me as we walk around and speak to others. As we understand what happened.

The days pass. The weeks pass. We do not return and no one else turns up at our door. I hear the stories and whispers on the streets about the orphans that have been found. The ones that were not murdered, were loaded up into a truck and paraded around the Old City before being dumped at its gates. Maybe Lulu is there, I wonder. Maybe she is there, and she hasn't found us. Every day I visit the house of Hind to see if Lulu is there. As you already know, she is not there. She never was.

But on my last visit to the makeshift orphanage, amongst the now familiar faces of the children, I see someone else. A face I recognise, quieter. Pale and thinner with her arm in a cast. But it was her.

'Suad?'

She turns to me and leaps up, wrapping her one fixed arm around me and crying.

'Suad. Your arm.'

She looks at the floor. She doesn't speak, so I carry on, 'Suad, the bracelet I promised Lulu. Do you have it so I can give it to her when I find her?'

Her face turns white.

'Suad, what is it?' She drops her arms from me and walks away. 'Suad, what is it? What happened?'

'She hasn't spoken since,' one of the volunteers whispers into my ear. She leads me gently by the arm, but I can't understand why she won't speak to me, her best friend.

'She is going to be reunited with her mother soon, but I'm afraid there was no one else that survived.'

I nod again to what is becoming a familiar tale.

'Why will she not talk to me?'

'Did you not hear? She had been there a few days. After the raid, she hid somewhere, but she hasn't told us where. But she saw it all happen and the poor girl was too terrified to come out in case they were still there. She had mud all over her and in her fingernails. They weren't going to let her in the ambulance, but an aid worker refused to let her out of his sight and accompanied her to the hospital and then to here. She must have seen so much, may Allah bless her soul.'

I sit there allowing it to sink in, imagining my Suad left all alone. Why didn't I insist she leave with me? I should have done; I was her best friend. 'Suad, before I leave, please tell me, did you hide the bracelet too?'

She nods her head. Her lips pressed together in silence.

'Where did you hide your things? Did you hide them in the house?'

She shakes her head.

'Was there a secret place in between the stones?' My voice is straining now, I am panicking that I will never find it.

She is shaking her head again.

I take her hands in mine and notice the earth underneath her nails. 'Did you bury them, Suad? Did you bury them in the ground?'

She looks straight at me and dips her chin forward slowly to her chest. Is that a yes? I plead with her to tell me. I am desperate. It is my last chance to try and undo what I have done. She becomes upset and starts to cry, covering her ears so she can't hear me. I am scared. I don't know what to do but I never meant to upset her.

That was the last time I saw her.

***

What I also keep from Layla is how her great-grandfather was taken and shot in the quarry that he built with his own two hands. The men who survived were taken and shot in the quarry. The one that belonged to her family. I hear the stories over the years from the mouths of others. I don't want her to live with that memory because before they took them from us, they had lives and happiness, and that's how she should remember them. And Suad, my dearest Suad. She kept that from her because that was another secret between us. There were some things only we could share. I don't want Layla to wake up in the night and see something else in the darkness. I want to leave her with Suad's light. Now Suad is gone and the hope of finding Lulu's treasure has disappeared with her.

Layla.
Chapter 7

AT HOME, THE RAINS fall, grey and hard on the red brick houses over the muddy green fields. Burning wood smoke billows from the chimneys, filling the air with a heavy woody aroma that makes me choke. At night I hold my children closer as the rain batters the brick outside, the sounds an ominous reminder that their precious lives are outside of my control.

During the night, I dream I am wearing my Tata's *thobe*. I have had this dream before. Once before, years before. In this dream, I am at Deir Yassin, but it is the darkest part of the night, a pathway lit by the faint glimmer of the distant moon. I hear my name being called through the trees; a child's voice. I run towards it, but I realise it is coming from the earth underneath my feet. I dig and dig but there is nothing there. I can see the Qadisha Valley mummies writhing in the earth, their bodies morphing with my children's.

I wake up and stare out of the window. I can't see the moon. Outside it is dark and silent. I walk to the wardrobe and pull out my Tata's *thobe*. I lay it on the bed. I study it with my fingers. I notice a tile in the *tatreez* I haven't seen on other designs I have been researching. It stands out because of its unfamiliarity and yet I feel like I have seen it before. I place the dress against me and look in the mirror. Fatima said it was like being with Tata again. I try to imagine how we were brought together. How Allah's plan is so meticulous in its timing. How this means something to me that I couldn't imagine. I feel connected to her and to my family and I can never repay her for how she has given them life again and made them alive for me in those moments she described. The everyday moments of them playing, laughing, stitching and eating together. Just as I am about to place the dress back, I notice some of the stitching unravelling on the sleeves. I tuck the threads inside to preserve it until I can find someone to help me fix it.

I tiptoe downstairs and sit by the French doors that look through the glasshouse and then out onto the garden. I see the skeletons of what looks like my dad's trees, silhouettes in the dark, and then my heart drops as I see a figure in the garden. I run round to the back and switch on the security light. A figure of a girl runs into the trees. I see the unmistakable patterns on the back of her dress and then I realise she does not belong here. She has followed me from Palestine.

I keep myself busy, distracted. A friend of a friend's children are struggling with their English GCSE. In truth, I don't think they are struggling with their exams. After a few sessions, I realise they are the most studious children I have ever met. They are dedicated, think hard, and ask great questions. Yet when I ask them questions about themselves, their responses are limited. I know they haven't always lived here, in England, and their heritage home is elsewhere, but it takes them weeks to tell me. I have seen it many times throughout my career, in the people I know, and in the families I know. There is an erosion of their identity to fit in. How other humans adapt and learn the language of another country, and how they assimilate is a testament to their intuitiveness and intelligence. However, I am concerned that this disconnection from their culture will come to wreak havoc on their adult selves. I want to live in a world where we celebrate and encourage children to hold on to their rich heritages and cultures. I give my students short stories to read, like V.S. Naipaul's *One Out of Many*. Where the protagonist, Santosh, travels out of India on the promise of an American dream and the securing of the elusive green card, but the closer he gets to his green card the more he loses himself. It resonates with me as I'm sure it does with many others.

It is more poignant for me now since I went back to Palestine. The girl still follows me here, but her figure is fading. As the weeks pass, I realise she must be a figment of my imagination. She turns up in my dreams, in the corner of the alleyways as I take my children to school. She disappears from view when the autumn light falls.

I often think of Fatima and of the treasure buried in Deir Yassin. Of my Tata's and uncle's treasure. I wonder if she can tell me who the girl in the photograph is. I know what I must do. I have to return. So, during the next holiday off school, I arrange to go back. This time I am taking my children. It is as much part of their future as it is my present.

Girl.

Part 4

IHAD NO CHOICE but to carry on. I had to keep going. I tried to stick carefully to the dirt road, realising that even under the shaded canopy the sky had darkened. Not a monsoon now, I thought. The rain would soak me, and I wouldn't be able to see ahead with the size of the raindrops here. The rain battered the roofs so hard I wondered how it would feel to be stranded out in one. And I knew that would make the track I was on almost impassable. Please God, don't send the rain yet. Help me get out of here first. And just as the words left my lips, I saw an opening in the forest up ahead, a break in the jungle. A wooden shack with an arrow pointing down and a simple sign painted in red signalled that I had arrived. I was so relieved I almost cried. I drove down towards the shack, which turned out to be a bar and reception area. I left my moped outside and was relieved to step inside just as the rain began to pour. 'Good timing,' I heard a voice say. A man was standing behind the bar putting glasses away.

'Oh yes, it was, thank God. I thought I would never find this place.'

'How did you?' he said, turning round and revealing his tanned face and receding hairline. He smiled through crooked teeth, and I couldn't help feeling a little jarred by his unkempt appearance and the fact that the place was empty except for us.

'Some travellers in Ko Phangan told me about it.'

He nodded his head, unsurprised. 'Well now you're here, sit down and order something to drink while we wait for the rain to pass. Then I will show you where you can stay.'

'Okay, thanks,' I said.

'And since we have some time, I may as well give you the house rules. Power is on between 7am and 9pm. No swimming at night. No swimming in the river behind us. It ain't safe. And after the monsoons come, the place is kinda cut off. You can't get out till it dries up so no funny business, like drugs or partying too much, cos there ain't no help coming here.'

I nodded uneasily, taken aback by his abruptness. 'Where are you from?'

'I'm from England, up north though. Further north than your accent gives away. What brings you here?'

'Just travelling. I am a writer.' Saying it out loud when it was so new to me felt fake.

'Yep, we get a lot of them here.'

I grimaced. Of course they do. I counteracted it. 'I wanted to travel and see the world.' It didn't sound quite so precocious – or maybe it did.

'Yeah, same with me. I'm still here, seven years later.'

'Do you like living here?'

He shrugged his shoulders. 'It's like everything in life. A path leads us somewhere and you stay till it takes you somewhere else. I can't imagine home now though. All that cold and grey skies.'

I nodded my head, thinking of it. But looking around, this place felt pretty dismal too. I was sure I hadn't come to the right place. I had visited far more beautiful places than this during my time here and I wondered what all the fuss was about. I decided I would stay one night because it must have been almost dusk, and I wasn't going to tackle the rainforest during the nighttime. I would stay one night and then when dawn came, I would get out of here and get back to civilisation.

I sat drinking my juice, staring out between the gaps in the wooden terrace as the rain poured. I walked around the back of the bar. It had an overhanging shade made of the same wood the bar was made of, a rickety platform. I stepped out onto it and saw the rain filling up the river behind us. There was a river that ran all the way along the back. I had seen a similar murky green when I was waiting for the bus but in the failing light, it looked almost black. It was deeper, running wild and fast. I stepped back from the platform into the supposed safety of the shack and sat down, watching it. A lump appeared out of the water. Wait. It wasn't a lump. It was a head. I rubbed my eyes. I must be seeing things. It was hard to tell with the smattering of rain and the mist rising off the dark water, but I saw something else. A tail flicked out of the water and then by the bank. It was a creature. Another one followed. Larger than my body in size, with heads like Komodo dragons. But I knew they couldn't be Komodo dragons as they were endangered and only to be found in Indonesia. I knew that from a documentary I watched once. I watched in horror as they bit their prey, and then just waited, skulking around it, waiting for it to die. They would begin to eat when it was too weak to fend them off. I shuddered at the thought. I jumped up as one slid past me and jumped into the river. I ran inside.

'Oh, you don't like them either. The locals hate the things.'

'What are they?'

'Monitor lizards,' he said, coming round from behind the bar and peering out towards them. 'Bad luck, the locals say. They bring evil with them.'

'Do you believe that?'

'Well, I ain't had much luck but can't say it's their fault. Just don't be swimming in the river. It ain't safe and if they do bite you, well…'

'There's no way to get medical help, yeah, I remember.'

'A fast learner, you are. And would you look at that, the sun's coming out. Let me show you where you can stay.'

I gulped down the last of my drink, eager to leave, and followed him out towards the side of the bar. It opened up onto a deck area on the beach. It had a barbecue area, fire pits and a shade that was strung with lights from each corner. Ahead of me was a stunning view. The cove was a curving U-shape with rocky hills to the left and right. Ahead was a calm stretch of ocean that rippled in towards the cove and ahead, there was nothing but sea. I could see the river running into the sea from the right. The river connected to the sea where the monitor lizards were swimming. I would probably stick to swimming on the left side to avoid one of them popping up next to me and giving me a heart attack. Or a nasty bite. Carl showed me a couple of huts on the beach, pointing them out with his finger and then he pointed up towards the rocky cliff. 'Or you can stay up there in one of them huts. They have a fantastic view of the sunrise and sunset.'

'I think that sounds good, thank you. But it will be only for tonight.'

He stopped and looked at me, 'What do you mean?'

'I have to leave tomorrow.' It sounded fake, clearly. There was nowhere I had to be. He looked at my clothes, splattered from the rainforest mud and the obviously tiresome journey to get here.

'You can't leave tomorrow.'

'Why?'

He pointed up at the sky. 'If it rains tonight, which it sure looks like it's going to, the track will be gone because the mud is heavy and wet. You can't leave here till it dries out a bit. It's impassable during the monsoon. You're lucky you even got in.'

'Well, if it doesn't rain again, I will make it the same way I got in.'

'As you like. But I'm a bit of a local now, I know this weather like the back of my hand.'

We were almost at the hut in the mountains. It was a wooden unit, slightly misshapen as though it was mostly made from flotsam someone had found on the beach. The windows were just holes in the two sides. No attempt had been made to provide any type of comfort. The bed was made of the same material, with a dark-coloured pillow set and quilt that looked as if it hadn't been washed in weeks. That was all there was to it. I was travelling, after all, I reminded myself.

'You might want to keep the door open at night or it gets a bit hot.'

'I will just put the ceiling fan on.'

He shook his head. 'Not after 9pm. The electricity is turned off. I have to keep the generator for the daytime. So, make sure you come and get some dinner. We have a barbecue tonight, my speciality. There's a few others staying here, so should be a nice crowd of about six or seven tonight.'

I agreed, I think, with a half-smile, although it was probably a grimace. I threw my bag in and followed him back down towards the beach restaurant where others had started to gather. Well, I wasn't going to stay in the hut for a minute longer than I had to. Plus, I was feeling hungry and a bit weak. I sat down in a chair and ordered off the menu. At least here there was something from home and the journey to the place had made me feel a bit off-kilter. I couldn't work out what it was. Was I homesick? I wasn't actually sure where home was. I had sold the flat in London. I hadn't lived in my childhood village for years. As the food was served, it gave me some comfort and as I began to unwind, I stared out to the sun setting in pinks and oranges on a silent beach with no boats tearing through the surf. A handful of people sat close by enjoying the same peace. Some were writing, others sketching on notepads or the easels that had been placed under a light, overlooking the magnificent view. I wondered what they were writing. Journals, future novels, travel guides? I pulled my notebook out. I realised why others might have loved this place. It wasn't for where they were staying or the ramshackle buildings that had been knocked up here. It was for the complete tranquillity. There were no boats. No full moon parties. No crowds of people. Dinner came and the night fell around us. We spoke and ate and sat until the lights went out.

Carl handed me a torch and I headed back across the soft sand, up through the rocks and sat on the edge of my bed. I shone the torch around the corners of my room to make sure nothing was lurking in the corners or had made a home in my blankets. I wasn't sure I was going to use the blanket, so I put my mosquito net around the frame of the bed, but it had gaps around the sides and wasn't long enough to protect from their nightly bites. Did they carry malaria here? I remembered that in my backpack I had some mosquito coils that I had picked up from a local stall back on the islands. I shone the torch in my bag and found them buried at the bottom. I lit them and left them on the table next to the bed. The coils of smoke streamed into the air, grey-green in the torch light. The torch began to flicker. I banged it on the side of the table. It went dead. Did the batteries die? I tried to untwist the back to see if I could tap the batteries out, but it must have been screwed on because it didn't budge. I banged it again to see if the light came on, but it was no use. Just a lighter in my bag and some matches. Why hadn't I brought a torch?! There was nothing I could do about it now. I tried to get some sleep, every now and then opening my eyes.

The room heated up quickly with the humid air that steamed down from the forest and tonight, there was no breeze. I could hear the buzz of mosquitos hovering around my ears. I kept batting them away, trying to hit the tiny creatures in the pitch black. The smoke from the mosquito coils filled the room and I was feeling lightheaded. I started to have vivid images flashing through my mind. Wait. Was I supposed to light them inside? What kind of smoke was pouring through the nets? I shot up and opened the door to the cabin, relieved by the expanse of space outside. I left the door open. I could hear the sounds of the jungle behind me. I closed my eyes, exhausted now but unable to sleep. Every time I closed my eyelids, I saw the shape of a dragon saunter in through the open door, its tongue flickering out of its mouth, tasting the air for prey. The lizards live near the cemeteries the locals say, they carry spirits with them. I had heard this story of spirits before. When I was a child. They had haunted me then. But that was a part of childhood I had forgotten. I had forgotten that I had been told those stories. That I had travelled to another place outside of England before. Faraway. In a land that I was told was home. I had come so far but missed it on the way. The hauntings had followed me here and had now morphed into the shape of dragons. I couldn't escape.

I shot up from my half-dreams and wandered outside. The blackness of the place was like I had never experienced. The darkness was impenetrable. I could not sleep in the tiny cabin with its walls crudely nailed together and the sound of the river snaking behind us, carrying the monitor lizards that sunk underneath its green surface, lying in wait for their prey. I imagined them silently stalking me, and every time I turned around, I could see their shadows in the dark.

A hammock was tied to the post. I tested it by putting half my body weight on it and then untwisted the fabric, emptying it of creatures I couldn't see in the dark. The moon was a slit in the sky offering a chink of light, reflected on the waves of the water. I could hear the sea swooshing back and forth as I rocked in the hammock. I couldn't close my eyes. I needed to be alert, and the only light was the light emanating from the sky shining on my view between the mountains, over the horizon.

I tried to walk down towards the beach. Maybe others couldn't sleep tonight and decided to congregate by the restaurant downstairs? Maybe someone had left a fire pit burning so we could see through the blackness of the night? Maybe a fire was kept burning to stop the lizards from wandering in? I took a few steps out of my cabin but lost my footing and slipped. The path was almost inaccessible at night because I couldn't see the loose rocks under my feet or where to go. I tried to look down towards the beach, but my view was obstructed by the twists and turns in the path. I thought I could make out the curve of sand, but it was as dark as the sea. The two merged together and I couldn't see any life down on the beach. No fires. No lights from the beach huts. It was as if I was completely alone. Isn't that what you wanted? My brain reminded me. Isn't that what you wanted? To be isolated and alone? Wasn't that where you were going to find paradise? Don't you remember where to find it? Have you forgotten it all?

I looked out over the black and had an overwhelming fear that the sun would not rise. If it did not rise and we were left in this perpetual darkness, what would happen? The creatures of the night would feast. The plants, starved of sunlight, would die within days. The world in all its beauty was so transient. The signs had been there all along. The tsunami warnings. The earthquakes. I think time has stopped. I think the light will never come.

I eventually fell asleep. In my slumber, I was transported somewhere else. It was vivid, as though I had been there before. The landscape was so vastly different from this one. Yet it wasn't England. It looked completely different to the rolling fields and red brick houses there. These houses were made of stone. A place I didn't immediately recognise but felt inherently familiar. It felt different. My body relaxed. I see someone, a familiar face. It is my dad's mother. I haven't seen her face for years, but I know it well. Her eyes are the same as mine. Her dark thin hair wraps neatly in a ponytail around her shoulders. Her smile shows her row of white, uniform teeth smiling at me. She is telling me a story. She is feeding me food I think I have tasted before. It is sticky and delicious. Are we together now?

'Not yet, my sweet, but don't forget the way. You already know it. Shush now and close your eyes. I will tell you a story.' It is a story I have heard before, but it seems like it was in another lifetime. Her voice soothes me.

'Are we in paradise?' I whisper in her ear.

'No, my sweet, we are not. It is not time for us yet. But don't forget, you know the way.'

She wraps her dress around me to keep my shoulders warm. The delicate stitching in the fabric, the symbols of her home, the symbols of her life stitched into the black fabric encompass me. For the first time, I feel safe, cocooned in her.

I awoke gently to the sunrise. The warmth of its yellow glow kissing the sea, signifying the day had begun, was one of the greatest mornings of my life. I placed my hands on my shoulders hoping to feel the stitching beneath my fingers. Hoping the scent of her would linger, the dreams of her would stay, because she had never visited me in my sleep before. I felt my bare shoulders, absent of her. I remembered parts of my dream. I wanted to hold on to them and escape back to that place, but I couldn't. With each breath of dawn air, the dream slipped further and further away until I lost her scent and the feeling of stitches beneath my fingertips. The food had lost its taste and her words morphed into my own voice inside my head.

Layla.

Chapter 8

YOUSEF AND HANNAH RUN ahead of me through the gates of Tata's old house. The courtyard is bare, and owing to the water diversions to the settlements, the gardens are barren. But they don't notice. Why would they? They have never known it as anything but this. I wonder if they will read my books someday and be transported to the place that it once was. How my Tata lived in it, how my childhood was shaped by it. They are welcomed by so many of our family members who have all travelled from the West Bank, Jerusalem and Betein to see us. It is a welcome I remember from my own childhood. That is why my arrival in Jerusalem with the film crew had felt so empty. It felt so at odds. I would write about the beauty of its scenery and the ancient stories the Old City was hiding, with its network of hidden caves underneath the city, with the walls built by the *jinn*, the winding limestone walls and the imposing gates of Jerusalem. But now I realise that as much as I love the landscape and feel almost at home here, it is the people that we return for. It is the people that make this place home, our home and now my children's home.

Yousef and Hannah walk into the room where Tata spent her last few years. I remember my dad. He would sit on the sofa next to her bed and spent many nights there keeping her company through the long nights when she barely slept. I am sad my children are visiting without them here. I can only imagine how it felt for my dad not to see her for the last year of her life. Especially after it happened like it did.

He spent a portion of his life in Amman. From his exiled home in Jordan, he could almost see Jericho. I remember standing in the same spot decades before. He was pointing out the mountains and rolling lands of a country that shared the same geography as his home. He would point out where he believed Jordan began and Jericho started. It wasn't a bad exile, to be so close; just a land crossing and he was home. In many ways Jordan's landscape mirrored Jericho. The fields and farming, the agriculture and produce. It was similar, almost the same. But of course, it never was home. It didn't have the same spring waters that fed into Jericho. It didn't have the same unique position. Jericho was a valley, the lowest and most ancient inhabited city in the world. It didn't have Jericho's mountains or its connections to Jerusalem. It didn't have my dad's stone house. It wasn't home to the quarry that built his family's wealth a hundred years ago. It didn't have his family in it. It wasn't home to the graves of those he had buried.

And then the land border closed. For the first time in his life, he could not visit her as he had done faithfully for his entire life since he left for the UK at eighteen. He hadn't gone longer than a few months without returning to see her. And yet the last time she was here on this earth he had been denied. Months of agonising document filling out, a countless number of calls to the Israeli embassy, frantic calls from the family urging him that with each breath, time was slipping away. He had stood out on his balcony staring into the land in the distance. The land that was his childhood home. That was her lifelong home. Separated by a land crossing and for all the money or time in the world, he could not get to her.

It was another defining moment to truly understand what exile meant and what effect it had on those still living. We stand here now together, all of us reunited like it is the easiest thing in the world, to cross a land border and to go home. But he had lost her without saying goodbye. She asked for him. But it was too late. He never made it. Those months apart were the hardest he had to bear, and it is a time he never got back. He read the Quran for her. She never learnt to read and write because she had become a carer for her mother, after Deir Yassin. She never had a childhood or an education. She had to take over and care for her mother and the family and so she had no time for it. Deir Yassin had altered their entire lives.

I imagine him in front of me now just as he was on our last trip. He sits in the chair and sips mint tea. His legs are tucked underneath each other, and he is barefoot in a plain T-shirt. He runs his fingers through his hair, even in old age only just speckled with the odd bits of grey in the dark brown, just as his mother's was. I see him belonging here more than anywhere else I have seen him before. As for me, I stand in the doorway, and I wonder, where is it I fit? If it is possible that I belong in two places and if my children do too. We are half Palestinian, people say. It reminds me of the *Half-Caste* poem by John Agard.

An when moon begin to glow
I half-caste human being
Cast half-a-shadow.

I am desperate to go and visit Fatima, but there have been skirmishes in Jerusalem and the West Bank is closed off from the city. Travel to Jerusalem is forbidden. Army tanks block the roads leading there. We must wait. As the days pass, I barely see the children. They are whisked off to Temptation Mount with Amira and Sumaya. They take them to visit the old archaeological site at the bottom of the mountain, they take them to visit elderly relatives who live in the stone houses they built decades ago, and to extended family and neighbours who welcome them with tea, fruits, biscuits and homemade zaatar bread.

I join them when we go and visit our family in Betein. It is the home of my aunt's family, who told me she was also from Deir Yassin. Her family live here. She moved down to Jericho when she married my uncle. We drive out of Jericho up the infamous mountainside roads and climb higher and higher into the mountain ranges until we reach Betein. It has always been a favourite place of mine, a place one would never imagine existing in Palestine. Its location means the climate is different. There is snow in the winter. Mild summers, a hardy landscape with expanses of land surrounding even the humblest of homes. Houses here are both traditional Palestinian homes and more elaborate designs based on differing architectural styles, from gothic arches and imposing windows on the larger mansions to Italian-inspired villas. My aunt's family live on a quiet edge of the village just past a vast stonecutting plant, where the stonecutting was moved to, after Deir Yassin. I have family who work there even today. It is a hard job, that of a stonemason. One of hard labour and immense skill. And a memory imprinted on the stone of what we lost and how. We pass the plant on the side of the road. It is quiet as it is closed now, but I can see the huge masses of stone lined up, ready to be cut.

We arrive at my aunt's mother's house. We are invited in by her sisters, Shams and Khulud. They have prepared tea and homemade pastries stuffed with dates. I wander to the windows overlooking the back of the house and out to the fields beyond. I can see my aunt's mother. She has a bag on her back and she is climbing over the rocky landscape, filling it with sage. The *marimia* is famous here, stewed in tea. I watch her and see Fatima in her. Both women are strong and active well into their old age. She looks as if she has always lived here and crossed these fields but I know from the documentary that that isn't true. There are Yassinis here too, in the hilltop towns, far from Deir Yassin.

The family next door are my Tata's sister's children. They come over and invite us to join them at their house that shares the same land. Jamila is there. She is older than Tata. Her eyesight is failing. She beckons us in and sits next to us on the floor. She tells us a story about Deir Yassin. She survived that day too, with Tata. She tells us that they hid under the dead animals in the barn until they had left. She too had seen it all.

I watch them make *mussakhan*, a traditional chicken, rice and onion dish flavoured with sumac from the crushed berries of the sumac trees. I scribble down the recipe in my notebook so I can recreate it at home with Hannah. I write it next to the story she tells me of Deir Yassin.

Afterwards, we walk through the town. Jamila stays behind, waving us off and telling us there will be *kunefeh* for dessert when we come back; one of her grandsons is out in the town collecting it for us.

We pass houses, many of them are quiet. In others, they are filled with families. I want to ask how many people still live here as it seems not all of the houses are inhabited. We walk past the stone-cutting plant. It falls down into the ground below us and the quarry has made a hole in the earth where it has been excavated.

We wander further into the town and there is a bakery on the corner. The streets are vaguely familiar. I'm sure I have been in a few of these houses before. We are invited in by our neighbours. They have maps of Palestine and their town names hanging on the walls. They have a small deer that lives on top of the roof garden. It is not safe in the fields. She shows me the olive trees that have been burnt down in the distance. They burn the olive trees that are older than the houses, older than their great-grandparents. I see charred stumps in the distance.

There are bigger houses here with grass-front gardens and cypress trees lining the edge of the streets. We pass by our family's old summer house. When the Jericho house became too hot in the summer, the family would come here. I recognise its positioning on the street; there are stone walls around it and an iron gate that leads onto the courtyard. It is a traditional Palestinian one-storey house made of stone, but it has fallen into disrepair. That is not unusual here. I ask whether they mind if I take a wander inside. 'Yes, go inside but don't go into the house. It isn't safe anymore.'

I walk through the courtyard.

I remember the garden from when I last visited. Twenty of us stayed in the house, sleeping on mattresses rolled out on the floor. We picked up fresh falafel and bread from the bakery and spent the evening in the courtyard together. That's where I heard that the snow falls so thick you can barely walk through it in the winter. That's where I heard about the hyenas that were planted there to kill the livestock and the deer in the field. I think of the tiger on the streets of Jerusalem. I have told you before, that fact in Palestine is always wilder than its fiction.

I leave my memories of the summer house behind as we walk back to Jamila's house. My aunt has come over with her daughters and together, we Yassini girls eat.

The sun sets in the sky. The children are tired. They are falling asleep on the sofa. Jamila invites us to stay and refuses to hear anything at all about us driving back down through the mountains at night. I agree.

Hannah falls asleep quickly. Her legs are tired after all the walking. Yousef takes a bit longer as he is being entertained by Khulud's stories. I wander out into the garden. The air has a chill. I pull my jacket around me. At nighttime, the place feels different. I can see lights on the hilltops. A turret in the distance. Car lights and torches light up the night sky. The stories I have written are now novels about this place. This exact place I am standing because it, too, is like nowhere else in the world. It is erased from maps and surrounded by settlements. The landscape is in some ways similar to Deir Yassin. Whenever I had pictured it before visiting, I imagined that the town that was stormed that night was like this one. Remote and surrounded, cut off from everywhere else. Perhaps because many towns were and still are raided and razed to the ground even today. I can see them coming over the hilltops. It could be here that it happens, even now. We could be asleep as they come in the night.

I go inside and find them all asleep on the sofas and the floor, covered in fleece blankets. Hannah is holding hands with my aunt. Even in her sleep, she does not let her hand go. There are seven of us in the main room. Everyone I love. I barely sleep. The place is no longer my idyll. I had reduced it to that as a child and even as a young adult. It is a place that is fiercely ours and it must be kept ours because if we leave there will be no Palestine left. I hear rumbling on the roadsides and the sounds of heavy trucks being driven through the streets. I cannot sleep so I ask Allah to protect us as we sleep, us and all those throughout Palestine, wherever in the world they are.

We awake early to pray and after a breakfast of homemade bread with boiled eggs, we hug them all and again, they don't want us to leave. They ask us to visit again soon and to make sure Hannah and Yousef come back. It is yet another visit where I feel like we just don't have enough time to spend with everyone and our goodbyes feel too rushed. I think we all could have stayed there with them for weeks. But yet again, we are on the move. Our time is running out.

We receive news that the roads to Jerusalem have reopened. We plan our to visit Al-Aqsa Mosque and of course, to visit Fatima and her family. At last. This time, I check I have the photograph. It is with me. We head to Jerusalem in a rented car that my uncle drives. It was his home here and it suited him to be driving through the streets he knew so well. As he drives, he tells Yousef and Hannah the stories of his homeland. He tells us of the neighbours we pass, of the shops his grandfather used to own in Jerusalem, of the land they had and the businesses, before. He shows them where their Sidu went to school and how he was the best student in his class which is why his family had pooled together to send him, the only one out of nine, to the UK for a top-class education. He tells them how Sidu was only seventeen when he arrived in the UK alone, homesick, missing his Tata and her cooking and the home he had left behind. I realise he never felt like England was home because it simply never was. Not in the way it is for me – although that was shifting.

We park just outside of the Old City and walk through the ancient streets. Yousef holds his uncle's hand as Hannah sits on his shoulders with the best view. He points out the high walls, the old streets, buying fresh fruits, breaking them into smaller pieces and feeding them as we walk. 'The best fruits in the world grow in these blessed lands,' he says, discarding the date seeds into the grass. The streets are bustling as they always are in Jerusalem with a cosmopolitan mix of locals in traditional Palestinian dress interspersed with tourists and religious groups.

We approach the Christian Quarter. In front of us, a heavily decorated church dominates the square. It is the church of the Holy Sepulchre. I stare at the wall next to it. I notice my uncle is looking at it too. 'I see them too,' he says.

'Who?' Yousef asks. And so, we tell him the story of the orphans that were abandoned in the city, in this very place, a lifetime ago. We take their hands and leave behind their stories that are carved into Palestine's history.

As we leave the Christian Quarter behind the call to prayer echoes through the *souk*. 'We are almost there,' my uncle says.

'We can make the midday prayers together.' He holds the children's hands, walking past the Israeli soldiers guarding the site. Just as we enter, the entrance opens up into the courtyards of the mosque. Ahead of us is the Dome of the Rock and behind archways and trees, Masjid Al-Aqsa. Its modest exterior opens out into a majestically decorated interior of chandeliers and rich red carpets. We sit together on the soft carpet as I tell the children of the famous night journey, where Prophet Muhammad (peace be upon him) was taken by a winged creature, the Buraq, from Mecca all the way here to this mosque. Then, from here, Angel Gabriel (peace be upon him) took Prophet Muhammad (peace be upon him) to the heavens above us. The children glance up to the roof. The prayers are about to start with the second *athan* and so we line up ready to pray. Afterwards, my uncle takes the children on a tour of Jerusalem whilst I walk the short distance to Fatima's house.

I arrive once again at the stone steps. '*Salam,* Fatima, I had to come back and see you! We tried to get here as soon as I arrived, but the roads were cut off.'

Suhair translates for me as Fatima clasps her hands around mine and kisses my cheeks. She is sending blessings upon us all and repeating her welcomes as she leads me through into the living room. The house is full. Women of all ages are sat around the main lounge area. Old sofas and chairs make a semi-circle inside the stone walls with impeccably clean stone floors. They are all stitching. One by one the women place down their *tatreez* and come and greet me with two or three kisses on the cheek, before making their excuses to leave. Suhair, the daughter of Fatima's neighbour, stays behind. She beckons me to come and sit next to her, showing me the *tatreez* she is making for her friend's wedding. She stitches with ease, her fingers slowly rethreading the different colours. Each cross stitch is worked into a shape. The shape then becomes a complete tile, and then she does it again and again. It is a long, dedicated process. I think of all the time it has taken to preserve such a tradition; a tradition that has made Palestinian women iconic throughout the world. Unified through their dress, they are visible to the world, wearing Palestine on their bodies. Palestine through its *tatreez*, through its ancient art, passed from mother to daughter through generations. She hands me thread and a piece of waste canva to try. I stare at it blankly. I am embarrassed at my lack of talent for it, and I am intimidated by it. She notices my expression. 'Don't look so worried,' she laughs. 'It isn't for everyone. My sister doesn't have the patience, but I have loved it ever since I was little. That is why I come and keep Fatima company. She teaches me how to do it. She is an expert around here.'

I am conscious that I have been waiting for a long time, so I delay it no further. I need to ask her about the girl in the photograph. I pull it out of my pocket and show it to her. I am about to speak, but I don't need to. As soon as she sees it, her eyes fix on the smiling face and tears run down her cheeks. She clasps it to her chest. 'Suad, my dearest Suad.'

It was my Tata as a child. The way she holds it against her heart, I realise it means more to her to have it. So, when she hands it back, I tell her to keep it. It is how she remembers Suad. And for me, the mystery is over. The darkest secret is in the open. The only reason my dad kept it from me was because of the horrors of that day. I know now that he was just trying to protect me. I can let go of the past. They are no longer buried under floorboards.

I lean over and notice a pattern. 'This is on my Tata's *thobe*,' I say, pointing to it, 'this one here.' I have studied it often, but I knew I didn't understand it the way they could.

'Ah, that is the almond tree,' Suhair says, 'One of my favourites.'

'I recognise it because it covers most of the dress.'

'The almond tree, it is famous in Deir Yassin,' Fatima says, 'We used to play under the almond trees.'

'When you go now, you will see them. We had almond trees around the house, by the roadside,' says Suhair.

'You have seen your family's old house?'

'Yes, it is still there. Someone else lives in it. Sometimes I take my grandmother and she collects her almonds. I wanted to stop taking her because it must be hard for her to return but she is determined to take her almonds off her tree. They belong to her. And so does the house, but this we know is not possible yet. *Insha'Allah* soon.'

I think of her collecting her almonds. I see my Tata there as a child again, running through the fields. I watch Fatima and she has drifted off, back to Deir Yassin, I imagine. I feel guilty for bringing it up again, so I change the subject. 'There is one pattern on the dress I don't recognise though. I have tried to research it online, but I cannot find it anywhere,' I say, reaching for my phone, scrolling past images of my children until I find the photographs I took of the *thobe*. 'Here,' I say, zooming into the image. 'Can you see? It is this one here.'

'I don't recognise it,' Suhair replies, 'Fatima, have you seen this?'

I take the phone over to Fatima, who is already pushing her glasses up towards her eyes and standing up from her chair. She is upright, tilting the phone so she can see it properly in the light. Her hands fall to her side, and she steps back into the chair. She fans her face with the fabric in her lap. I give her a few moments to catch her breath. Suhair puts her fabric down and comes over to see if she is okay. 'What is it, Fatima? Do you need anything?'

Fatima regains her strength and sits forward, holding my hands in hers and pointing to the image on my phone.

'The tile, it is from Deir Yassin. There is a stone wall there. A place they used to play near as children. Your Tata has stitched it into her *thobe*.' Suhair pauses as Fatima speaks to her in Arabic. 'Can she see the whole dress?'

'Yes, I brought it with me. I was going to ask my aunty to do some repair work so it's back at her house in Jericho.'

'Could you bring it back for her to see?'

I look at Fatima, asking her in breathless tones, repeating the same phrase.

Suhair looks at me. 'Please, it is important she sees her old friend's dress as soon as she can.'

I agree to bring it back as we are interrupted by the children at the door with my uncle. They have finished their explorations, which I find out was a stop at all my uncle's favourite food stalls, the places of the greatest stories in Jerusalem's history, and now here. The children come inside and take over the space with their exuberance and playfulness. They sit with Fatima as she hands them bowls of grapes and sliced watermelons that her sons had prepared earlier.

Fatima's sons return with freshly ground coffee, immediately leaving it to come and meet the children, so Suhair serves it up. Fatima is with us, but she keeps looking at the image on my phone. She keeps it in her hands and occasionally smiles. I don't know what it means. But for now, I revel in the present. Their home behind the limestone walls is alive with the aroma of roasted ground coffee, cardamom and the stories my children will tell theirs.

Before we leave, I agree to return to Fatima's tomorrow in the late afternoon with Tata's *thobe*. She pleads with me not to forget.

Girl.

Part 5

MY DREAM OF HER dissipated into the day. I couldn't capture any of it in the brightness of the day. I looked down at the mosquito coil wrapper on the floor and picked it up to read the back of it, now I could see. Do not light in enclosed spaces. For outdoor use only.

I packed my mosquito net up and walked down for breakfast. My ankle was sore from the fall last night and I think my back was grazed too as it stung in places. I took off my sandals and walked along the surf. I rolled up my trousers and waded into the sea. It was cool against my body. I wandered further into the deep. My clothes were heavy around me, but the refreshing coolness of the water was too much to resist. I dipped my head under the water and opened my eyes. I rose out of it and took a deep breath and collapsed on the sand as the waves rolled in and out. The sand stuck to me, and my clothes wrapped tightly around my skin, but I didn't care. I had made it through one of the longest nights of my life and I only had one thing on my mind. I needed to get out of here.

I went back up to my cabin to change and since no one had witnessed my early morning swim, I didn't feel like I needed to explain it to anyone. By the time I went down again for breakfast, a few were already there, ordering. I waved and they waved back and went back to reading the menu. I saw Carl coming to take their order.

'Carl, can I get out?'

He looked at me, slightly startled. His clothes hadn't been changed from yesterday and looked crumpled, as though he had slept in them. He scratched his head before answering. 'Good morning to you as well.'

'Sorry, it's just, it didn't rain last night so –'

'It isn't like I have taken you prisoner here,' he laughed.

I laughed nervously. I felt as if I was so far away from where I was supposed to be that I didn't want to stay a moment longer. I had already packed my few belongings and had no interest in going back up to the mountain cabin, which now, as I glanced back, looked precariously positioned on the cliff edge.

'Sorry, miss, but it did rain during the night. It tipped it down just as I said it would. It's too dangerous to try and get out now. It's going to take a few days to dry up.'

'What? I stayed up all night. It didn't rain.'

He looked at me and then looked back towards the shack. The mud was splattered up the sides, and the path that was there yesterday was a boggy mess.

'That's the thing with paradise. It has its downsides too. But there are worse places to be trapped than here. Most people would dream of it. What do you fancy for breakfast?'

I left him and ran over to where I had come in the day before. He was right, the mud was so thick my legs sunk almost immediately down to my knees. How did I not notice the rain last night? I was awake, wasn't I? I panicked and tried to pull myself out, covering my hands and smearing it onto my face as I tried to wipe the hair strands away that were irritating my face. I was completely stuck. I choked back tears but managed to pull one leg free, and then another. I didn't want anyone to see my stupid mistake, so I walked back behind the cabins and changed in the outdoor changing rooms and showers that were usually reserved for those staying in the beach hut that had no bathroom facilities. Since I was leaving, I had my backpack with me, so after a quick change I went back into the restaurant.

'Okay, so you were right,' I said, after having calmed down considerably in the shower. Last night had thrown me off so much that I think I panicked. I realised there was nothing I could do but ride it out.

'Well, breakfast?' Carl said. He looked at my clothes and knew I had changed, but he didn't say anything about it. I think he could tell I was a bit lost. So instead, I ordered breakfast and waited to pass the longest days of my life.

The days and nights.

Almost a week had passed. I wiped the rainwater off my moped seat and rode through the rainforest to get back to the main road. The main road that would lead me back to the train station at Surat Thani so I could get to Bangkok. I was heading straight for the airport. I had memories of my childhood. Her face, the familiarity of her clothes and the feeling I had that night on the mountain cove. Everything in me ached to go. I had not found paradise here. But I think I knew now where I had to look to find it.

Fatima.

Chapter 8

MY SONS WANT TO take me out to the beach. They spent weeks organising the pass to allow us to travel beyond Jerusalem. I don't want to go but they say the sea air will be good for me. I don't like to leave the Old City. The truth is, I haven't gone far since I arrived as a child. I see too much. The history tells me too many stories I don't want to remember. They worry about me as I wander out sometimes. I go to the places I used to go to find her. They gently take the *thobe* I am working on from my hands and take me away from my limestone walls. 'Remember the tiger, Mama?'

I nod my head. The story of my son's miraculous survival. I am not surprised. All of us alive are miracles, especially here. It reminds me of when they were young. I didn't tell you much about that time. I will tell you now.

I married a boy who was also from Deir Yassin. He was at the prayers with his father that morning. Afterwards, he lived in the refugee camps with his father. It was just the two of them left. He didn't speak often. So, his father brought him a pen and a notebook, and he used to mostly write down his thoughts and became a poet. His poetry never made enough to feed us, so he had a job working at the clothes *souk* with one of his uncles, but his poetry fed his soul and through it, he transported us back to the time of our childhood. That is his poem there, on the wall. It sings the song of our homeland and one we have never forgotten, and the people.

Seedlings left upon the soil,
Sink deep into its darkness.
Do not fear,
We will return under your glorious shade.

We shared the same past, the same history and the shared love for a home that once was. And so together we grew another home.

When I became pregnant, I fell into weeks of sheer panic. I was not strong enough to protect a baby inside me or the body of a newborn. All the memories of what happened the decade before came flooding back. I couldn't sleep at night, unsure of what the night would bring and that my unborn child would be taken away from me before I had the chance to meet them. But I had no choice. Not many of us did. There were few places to go and even fewer places with no money and a parent to care for.

That evening I was stitching with Dana, my neighbour from next door, who was a similar age to me. Dana had a young boy and was pregnant with her second. 'How do you know if you can keep them safe?' I asked, exposing my deepest fear to her.

'We cannot, sister, that is up to Allah, but we must live. What is this life if we live in fear of it being taken away? We have been told that it will be taken from us, they are lent to us for a specific time and only Allah knows when that is.' She reached over and grabbed her little boy who was engrossed in building a tower from some empty milk cartons. 'And I intend to enjoy every minute of their blessed lives.'

He protested and she let him go back to his building. I often think of her and how I marvelled then at the love a mother could have for her children. I had never experienced it before, so to me, it was a feeling I couldn't yet comprehend.

That ended on the day that I met my Mohammad. I named my sons after my brothers and intended to have more to name them after everyone we had lost. But there he was, my Mohammad. He arrived on a day that was as ordinary as any. We didn't have time to make it to the hospital, so he was born in my great-grandfather's house and one of the elders who lived close by was called on by my husband. They say you forget giving birth, but I have not. It was the first time that I felt connected with him.

During my pregnancy, it was alien to me, this life inside of me growing and changing my body. I didn't feel like I had the ease my mother had, being a natural mother when she was young. Fear had taken over and he had become another thing to protect. But as he breathed his first breath and wailed loudly in the house, his dark brown eyes opening for the first time, I felt what it meant to have something to live for. It gave me a new lease of life, something to wake up for in the mornings, something to build a better Palestine for. He was swaddled to me day and night and grew next to me as I worked in the house, preparing dinners for when his baba was back. I took him to Al-Aqsa Mosque from a few weeks old so he would grow with the sound of the *athan* and prayer inside his ears.

When he began to crawl, I let him loose on the courtyards there so he could feel the stone beneath his hands and from then on, I would tell him how his family owned the stone that built his city.

I tried to savour every breath my baby took, never knowing when it could be his last. I was already busy with feeding and changing Mohammad, barely sleeping through the nights, and so the second pregnancy passed quickly. I realised that in motherhood, I didn't have the luxury of time to think. There was an urgency to life. I had to keep a baby alive and fed and changed and it took up all of my time. I relished the busyness of it all. I saw a shift in Mama too. She would hold the boys and smile again, a smile I hadn't seen since before. I am not sure what she thought, perhaps they reminded her of her boys but I discovered a new way to love and a new way to live that gave us hope for our future.

Mama seemed to be happier during the last years of her life. I don't know if it was because she knew that her life was coming to an end and she would be reunited with her babies again, or if it was because the grandchildren had reignited a maternal love and she realised she still had some left to give. She would hold them and be next to them, always watching them wherever they went; she wouldn't let them out of her sight. She would make us *marimia* tea when they had a tummy ache and show me all the things she had learnt as a mother. Her death came as a surprise to me as she was still quite young, although she looked as though she had aged more than I had. It was the grief, I knew. It had broken down her body irreparably and more importantly, her spirit. She died knowing we were rebuilding Palestine. Stitching its flags onto our dresses and dreaming of when we would return. She died just before the war in 1967 and I was relieved she didn't have to live through that. After that blow, when thousands more Palestinians lost their lives, homes and livelihoods, it became harder to envisage our return home. We had already been absent from our lands for decades. But there would be time for all that. In the meantime, we had many thousands more refugees who needed us.

We took in families who had nowhere else to go. They arrived much as we did that day barely two decades before, with only the clothes on their backs and their lives shattered. Because we understood what that felt like, we rallied around and made extra clothes from the scraps of materials and threads we could find. We scraped together more food to feed hungry mouths. We had become experts at it now. We stayed up through the dark nights with the sounds of war outside the windows and soldiers' boots stomping through the alleyways. I was no longer a child. Now I was a mother, and it fell to me to be brave and strong and to tell the refugee children trying to fall asleep on our stone floor, that they would be okay and that they would have a home soon and, in the meantime, they had a home with us.

There was always talk of justice. Of how they could get away with it and continued to get away without any worldly justice. But we had our own. *That day shall we set a seal upon their mouths, but their hands will speak to us, and their feet will bear witness to all that they did.* (Surah Yasin, Qur'an). Allah is Just.

They don't understand why we stay because they don't understand that it isn't just about the houses we live in and inherit or the land that is ours that has been stolen from beneath us. The land is ours and it is rightfully so, but it is more than that. This land is linked to something greater. The night journey of the Prophet (peace and blessings be upon him), where he ascended to paradise from these very streets in these very skies. The skies above Jerusalem will crack open on the Day of Judgement and the angels will descend here. Jesus (peace be upon him) will return to this land. All of the Prophets will pray behind Prophet Muhammad (peace and blessings be upon him) at the mosque that is on our doorstep and one we must protect until the end of time. Of course, they don't understand why we stay, because they don't understand that it isn't just about what is beneath our feet. It is about what is above us, high, high above the skies. Allah is with us. We belong here and we will never leave.

As we wait, we see there are always people worse off than us. There were always those who had lost more or had to live with less and so we were grateful for the blessings bestowed on us. We were grateful for the nights when we slept without fear. Where we slept not feeling the pangs of hunger in our bodies. When we had days of peace. We were grateful for the Palestinians around us, for our shared unity and community; for what we were trying to build together, and we were united. United in a way where it didn't matter where we came from. We were Palestinians no matter where in the world we ended up. We had our children, we grew our families, we stitched out of view of the windows, out of sight of the passing army, and we fed the men sitting in the courtyards of Al-Aqsa Mosque. There was plenty of work for us to do. It was in memory of those we had lost, it was in the hope of our future that we had to fight every day for. But we kept it alive through our stories and poetry and through our clothes and our flags. We wore the *thobes* on our bodies and showed the world that we weren't just mothers and the mothers of martyrs. We could wear our Palestine on our bodies and stand with our men. Even the news images from around the world showed others joining us. The handstitched *thobes* made by Palestinian women like us were being worn by others in a show of solidarity.

I had no time to reminisce about the past; that would come later in my quiet years. At that time, it was about survival. It was about rebuilding our Palestine.

And when I look back now, those were my happiest years, after. After it happened. That's why I want to tell you these memories because those years were lost in caring for the tiny bodies of newborns, in nurturing life and raising them in the streets of their home. In telling them of their past and the history, etching their history and lives into the stone houses. They are marked with their children's carvings and childhood memories and height marks on the stone. Yet even during those days, there were mornings just before wakefulness had fully infiltrated my body when I woke up dreaming that I was in the fields of Deir Yassin. In those mornings, I could smell the fruit ripening in the trees and smell the blossom from the almond trees in the air.

Many stories I have read about Palestinian refugees are that when they wake up, they dream they are in their fields back home, in their gardens, in their houses. We are all spread around but together we are building. And I know from my baba about our work and how we build. If we build it properly it will last far longer than us.

My memory fades as the present appears.

The seaside town glitters in its modernity. A metropolis built on the foundations of other people's homes. And I see their semi-naked bodies lying on the warm sands as the ocean hisses at their feet. Do they know what lies underneath them? Do they know what this is built upon? I find it hard to separate the two places, but they do not. I will not set foot on the bodies of those slaughtered underneath. I will not forget the mass grave that lay underneath the site. Scattered throughout Palestine are the shallow graves of those whose lives were robbed, and their earthly bodies buried underneath its façade. It is not a matter of just being Palestinian. It is about being human. I imagine that wherever it is I end up in this life of mine, I will never be one of those bodies resting on a site where the sand underneath hides the atrocities that were committed in our living memory. Tantura. They have found it now, I heard. The archaeologists have scanned it from the skies. They have seen the graves underneath it. It reminds me my memory is as sharp as it's ever been. They can't bury these atrocities from our memory. I tell them of my earliest memories here. They see it now and they take me home. There is barely anywhere in this country left to put our feet.

It has killed half of the day for me, so I try to rid myself of the feeling that I carried at the beach. I think of what we have buried, and I want it back in my hands. I can almost feel it now, between my fingertips, just within reach.

Layla is coming back tonight with Suad's *thobe*. Her Tata, my Suad, made it and she has now inherited it. I will ask her tonight how she lived and loved. She had many children and grandchildren, so that makes me feel at peace. I cannot believe that I have seen her granddaughter now. She had gone on to live a long life since that day back at the orphanage and I am proud of her. I am proud that she has made her granddaughter a part of our future, just like I intend to with mine.

There is a knock at the door and Layla is there with the *thobe* in her hands. I take it from her and lay it gently on the table and sit down to look at it. I run my hands over the stitches and imagine Suad's hands, night after night, stitching it. It is covered in almond trees. But the tile Layla did not recognise, I recognised immediately. They are the patterns I made in the stones as a child. I know exactly where it is. It is just next to the family almond trees. Suad has made me a map. A map to our treasure.

I start to roll my lips. The sound rings out loud and clear.

'Mama, what are you celebrating?' Ibrahim asks.

'My Suad has made this for me.'

'What do you mean?'

'I mean it is a map to something she buried back in Deir Yassin all those years ago.'

'Are you sure, Mama?'

'Am I sure! Look at it. It is as clear as day. Look.'

I show him the stitches and I am explaining to him that he needs to take us there. Mohammad is home, he will come too. And Layla.

The children follow her inside.

'And the children?' Ibrahim asks cautiously. He looks at Layla. I see on her face a mix of fear and surprise. A hint of disbelief in my treasure map.

She agrees but only because my eyes are pleading with hers. She will come. I know it. She also wants to know the truth.

'But, Mama, you haven't ever been back. Are you sure?'

'I don't have much time left on this earth and this is what I have been searching for. I haven't asked you boys for much. Please grant it to me. It is the last thing I will ask of you.'

I don't know how else to make them leave right now at this moment. My sons talk with Layla and amongst themselves. I feel like a child, waiting to know my fate. I can't take it anymore. I leave as they discuss it and I go and strap myself into the car. They will take me, or I will drive myself.

They rush down after me. 'Looks like we don't have a choice,' Ibrahim says to Layla. 'But you do.'

She straps the children into the back seats. She puts her hand in mine, and I hold it the whole way. She clasps her hand around my palm. It is just how Suad would hold my hand, subconsciously stroking my palm with her thumb. I close my eyes and the car pulls us away from the Old City, from my home, to one I used to know.

We arrive at Deir Yassin. I open the tinted windows so I can see the afternoon light. I see the people that are living in our houses. The fig trees are now stumps around the village. We drive through, past a psychiatric hospital. Surrounding it is a green iron fence, but behind the fence are not the standard clinical gardens you would expect to see at a hospital. Instead, the land beneath us rises and falls, it is uneven beneath my feet. We pull over and stand next to the schools. They are quiet now as the students have left for the school break. I see a bench overlooking the horizon. I rest. My mind cannot see what it has been remembering for the last seventy-five years. Instead, I see a site, cut up, used for something else. Where am I? I can't place myself. I don't know where our home once stood. I turn around and notice Layla is looking through the green gates. I walk towards her. Her eyes are scanning the houses and grounds. There are houses behind the green iron fences. They are our homes; Yassini homes. Their stone is instantly recognisable. Their gardens are scrub lands now, unattended. But the almond trees still stand in some places. I too look at the ground and wonder, what is underneath it? I am starting to remember the position. The horizon, the top of the hill. I walk over to where I was stood that day and I have a vantage point over the town beneath us. The towns surround us.

The day plays out in front of me, and I see Lulu face down in the earth. I close my eyes and will the image away. This time when I look, she is smiling and running over the fields. There are others too. Spectres of them as my mind slips from the past to the present. I see the children I used to play with from school. I can hear them laughing and playing now. I can hear the sound of life inside the houses of pots and pans, of washing and running water, of the plants being watered and harvested. Of footsteps of the Yassini girls as they harvest our fields. I see them again now, Suad and I, my sister and mother, through the open back doors sitting in plain sight, stitching their *thobe*s and drinking *marimia* tea. I know the twins are with my father. I see them standing next to him, one on either side, identical as they walk towards us, their hands covered in limestone dust as if they have been walking through powdered snow. We are all together again.

Layla has the *thobe*. I follow the almond trees on it. They lead to the ruins of a house, to its walls. We keep walking, the children run behind us, and I can hear their voices in the air. I look for the tile. Eternity. I inscribed them on the walls as a child. We must be close. I see the almond tree at the top of the hill. I see Suad call me to it. Our homes are just past it. I find the stones of what used to be our living room walls. Now they are broken. But in a half-crumbled wall, I see a pattern. There are unmistakable zig-zag carvings across the bricks. I go back to the *thobe*, after the zig-zags, there are palms and trees, and in the centre of the dress, a tree of life. I know now instinctively which tree it is.

We walk together, Layla urging me to slow down but I cannot. I am too eager after all this time to find my sister's bracelet. Suad's *thobe* is leading me to her again. She is leading me to find what I asked from her, all those years ago. I move faster. My heart beats inside my ears and my face is flushed from the heat. I can hear my sons; they are calling me to slow down but I don't stop. I look down at the *thobe* and see its position. I am in the centre tile, at the tree. I run my fingers over the stitches to see if there is anything I have missed. I look down at the soft soil beneath the old tree. The tree stands firm, unwavering, its branches spread out further than they did when I was a child. It has become stronger, its roots more deeply entrenched in the soil.

My sons are with me now. I plead with them to dig, to unearth what is hidden in the ground. Layla looks worried. I can tell because she sends the children to investigate something further afield, but they do not want to go. They know we are on a treasure hunt. I see it in their eyes. But Layla does not want to unearth what is buried in the ground. I can tell. She wants to leave it. I have not come this far to leave now.

My sons dig. The heat around my heart intensifies and I loosen the scarf that is wrapped around my neck. The afternoon breeze cools the sweat against my skin. My eyes are failing in the falling light. I blink to remove the dots that keep appearing in my vision. I can smell the soil as it is unearthed, and I smear it into my hands. I turn over my palms. They suddenly look like they did that day, all those years ago. I am leaning next to the tree, and I can see them digging. There seems to be nothing but soil. 'Keep going,' I tell them, 'we will find it,' but I remember that no one else knows what we are looking for.

Ibrahim is telling me to give up and go back to the car. I can't imagine how my body will move slumped by this tree. But Mohammad keeps digging. He has always been determined, ever since he was small. Just then I hear something hit the hard soil. It is a box and around it there is fabric. My sons, and even Layla, are here now on their knees. Her children too. They are pulling things out of the ground and looking around in bewilderment. They are pulling out objects from the mud that I can't quite make out. My eyes see the horror in Layla's eyes as she lifts one from the soil. It is the shape of a small baby, a newborn. It can't be older than that, judging by its tiny form. There is an infant under the soil. I see the Qadisha Valley mummies. I should be more shocked. I take deep breaths and press my hands into the ground around me, readying myself to stand, to ask them to stop. But as I struggle to voice my words, my eyes adjust. Mud is being brushed off the baby. But it is solid. It is as solid as plastic. It is a child's doll. It is wearing a dress of black fabric, and the fabric is stitched with embroidery in simple patterns; a child's work.

Other objects are rubbed down and drawn out from their resting place. There are pieces of *thobe*s and a purse with old coins inside. And then a box, a wooden box. It is thick with damp soil, so they scrape it off and find the opening. They open the box and inside there is a pearl necklace, a few gold rings, a lock of hair and underneath it all, the bracelet.

I reach out and pull it from the box as the others search the soil around us. It is yellow gold and embossed with zig-zag patterns around its circumference. It is smaller than I remember. Inside, the name Layla is carved. It is my Lulu's bracelet. I go to slip it onto my wrist, but it is too small. I want to take it to her. 'Lulu, I have found it. My dear Lulu, forgive me. I have it now.'

I see them all now. No time has passed. They are as youthful as they were that day. The twins are here, Ibrahim and Mohammad. I call their names, but they are already by my side. I see Suad, she is holding my hands.

It is in front of me now. It is bigger than I remember; a castle rising from the ground built in stone. The children are laughing again, and they run around the fields. The gardens are springing back to life in front of my very eyes. The grass is green, lush and soft underneath our bare feet. The trees are no longer stumps but solid trunks, and all of them bear fruit of figs or almonds. But where is Lulu? I call her name. I search for her and then, at last, I find her. A hand reaches out to me. A silk *thobe* embroidered with red stitches around the cuffs reaches out, a wrist adorned with gold, and I slip the bracelet onto it. It is a perfect fit. Her hand pulls me to follow her. I see her dark honey-coloured hair fall down the back of her silk dress. I am going with her now. It is time.

I look behind me. For a moment I wonder if I can leave them behind, but I see there is no one left behind. They are playing; it is like we haven't left. There is Mohammad, Ibrahim and Suad there, and they have their children with them. Their children are playing on the grounds we used to call home and they have our stories and our history, and they will take it and pass it on, so we are not forgotten. The earth lies beneath their feet and their roots have grown from it. I have passed on everything I could have passed on. My babies are now men, and they will inherit our homes, our land and our heritage. And to their children too, and to their children after that. Our houses made of stone will last for their lifetimes. And I will see them all again. Gold lasts longer than stone.

And so, I drift away, surrounded by those I love and those that I have lost, and we are together again.

Limestone is caused by the precipitation of seawater over millions of years. If we build it properly, it will last well after we are gone. But there is something more that we live for in this world. *All that the souls could desire, all that eyes could delight in* (43:71), a place where our homes, gardens and rivers are for eternity.

Layla.
Chapter 9

I ARRIVE AT FATIMA'S house with the *thobe*. Hannah and Yousef have begged to come and so I take them. I would rather steal away with them and keep them safe. But I am realising that keeping them safe is out of my control. They will either be with us here, in the lands throughout the earth, or they will be in paradise. As the world becomes more tumultuous and I learn what other people can do to each other, these are the only options I have. Fatima and many like her live a life of hope and life after such trauma. They live fully and they build for generations to come in this life and the next. I want to inherit this from them, and it pushes me to see things in a way I never have or could. It is the hardest journey I have taken in my life so far.

Fatima answers the door, smiling. She calls me Suad. I do not correct her. I can't imagine how it must be to be visited by someone who looks like an old friend you lost seventy-five years ago. I wonder why the two of them had never met up again after. But I was also starting to understand that in order to live, a life needed to be built away from the old one.

Fatima takes the *thobe* from my hands. Her eyes light up and her lips begin singing out loud. Her sons rush over, and I back off, slightly bewildered and slightly fearful, but I am not sure why this feeling rushes over me. The next part is a blur. The dress is a treasure map. The way she looks at it and scans the stitches between her fingertips and her eyes, I know she is absolutely sure. Who am I not to believe this? I know the truth in Palestinian stories, and I have long known that this is a land built upon the most extraordinary of those. I know very little of the past they shared. She rushes to the car and refuses to leave it. She wants to go to Deir Yassin. They say I don't have to go. I have the children with me. But I climb in and sit next to her and hold her hand. It is the least I can do for her. For her and Tata. This is another time I need to swallow my fear.

As I sit there, Mohammad is reading the document in the *thobe*. He turns to me. 'Your Tata, she stitched the deeds to the land inside her dress.'

'Which land?'

'It is the land they owned in Deir Yassin. Where their house was, their business. It is now where the psychiatric hospital stands. Your family own that land.'

We all look out of the windows as we drive through and out of the city. Behind the stone walls of its modest houses. The grand city, sprawling and ancient, home to millions of stories and our family stories make up part of them.

I see three women a decade or so younger than Fatima carrying large, covered trays in the *souk* towards Masjid Al-Aqsa. 'That smells like *maklouba*.'

'It is,' Mohammad says, 'they have been bringing it every

day since I can remember to feed those who are guarding Masjid Al-Aqsa.'

'Not just years, brother. It is the dish of victory dating back to when Salahuddin conquered Jerusalem in 1187. Before then, it was called *baitenjaniyeh* as the main ingredient was aubergine.'

'There is still a debate as to which is better. My favourite is aubergine.'

'Cauliflower,' Yousef and Hannah answer. 'But I will eat either...' Yousef adds.

I laugh.

'There have been many times it has been used to serve and feed the people who are protecting the sacred ground at Al-Quds, especially when there are sit-ins, or when there is trouble. Another strong Jerusalemite, Hanadi from the Halawani family, invited the worshippers who were banned from going into the mosque to have *maklouba* with her relatives at the Chain Gate or Bab Al-Silsila. It is her way of being part of her city.'

'We are all part of Palestine. Our daily job is to fight for our homes and our land. You know they have offered us millions to buy the stone house that was our great-great grandfather's. Millions. And not just because of its prestigious position in the Holy City, but also because underneath it, caves and tunnels lead all over the city.'

I think of the tunnel in the stone in the wall. If you live in these houses, you can access the entire city.

'Maybe that was where the tiger came from!' Yousef joins in. 'Maybe he walked through the tunnels.'

'Imagine, Yousef, what else there is there. He could still be there now but maybe he was fed too much *maklouba* and so he didn't want to eat my brother that night.' We all laugh.

It is in my nature to avoid the evil that exists in the world. I would rather pretend it didn't happen or that it was detached from me. But what I had failed to see was that it gave others a purpose to strive and to live and to help others. Throughout all the stories that were unfolding, each and every one had hope and life inside of it. From Hind rescuing the orphans, or women stitching the Palestinian flags and keys in their dresses in the darkness, to the mothers raising families, to the women cooking *maklouba* on the gas-lit stoves to feed the worshippers at Masjid Al-Aqsa. From the women who clothed the refugees when they arrived with nothing except what they were standing in, in feeding others, in taking care of one another, in the journalists telling the world what was happening, in the prisoners who refused to leave the country but instead were incarcerated in it. Those striving with their art, confiscated off walls and imprisoned for their writing. They were forging their own history and their own belonging to Palestine.

I believe that true talent emerges in defiance of all the forces of oppression, subjugation and denial. Sliman Mansour.

We approach a checkpoint entering Jerusalem. 'Don't tell them we are going to Deir Yassin,' Ibrahim says. 'Don't mention the name.'

The Israeli soldiers in military uniform have guns hanging over their shoulders. I notice Yousef looking at the guns.

'Are they real?' he asks.

'Yes, Yousef, they are.'

They glance inside the car and leaf through the passports and documents that Mohammad has handed over to them. They wave us through.

We arrive at Deir Yassin. The houses are traditional Palestinian houses, made from the same limestone that was cut from both of our family's quarries. They took them back and shot them in the quarry. It feels different without the film crew; I feel more exposed. Last time the Israelis brought guns. The amputated trees line the edge of the village. They were fig trees. The streets are in use. There are cars parked in front of the houses. The almond trees are still here. The houses are still here but other people inhabit them. Built from the limestone the entire city is built with.

Yousef stays behind in his seat. Hannah is with Ibrahim, so I turn to Yousef and kneel by the side of the door. 'Are you okay?' I ask him, as he looks around.

'Is it safe?' he asks.

'I wouldn't bring you if I thought it wasn't. But you don't have to get out if you don't want to.'

'What about the people that died here? What if I see something?'

'There are old homes here that you can see. A few of them used to belong to our family. To your great-great grandma and grandpa. They used to have businesses here and farms. Would you like to come and see where your family were from?'

He unclips his seatbelt and I hold his small hand in mine. It was a story I hadn't ever wanted him to know but it was part of his history as well as mine and it wasn't mine to keep. We also had the privilege of leaving whenever we wanted to. Palestinians do not. They live their lives like this.

We wander hand in hand, looking around. I look at Fatima. She looks different here. Belonging perhaps, with a vigour I haven't seen before. She is walking around, able-bodied on the uneven ground, searching for the details that my Tata stitched into the dress.

'Layla, Layla,' I hear her call and jog over to where she is standing.

'Yes, Fatima?'

'No, I was calling my sister. I see her,' Fatima says, pointing over towards the horizon. I can't see anyone.

I stop thinking, interrupted by the sounds around us. The birdsong is broken up with howling and singing. The voices are coming from the grounds behind the gates of the hospital. I encourage Yousef to go and join Ibrahim and Hannah in the other direction.

I walk towards the sounds coming from inside the green gates. Inside the green gates, I can see figures. I can't make out what is happening. Are people living inside the houses? I can see them moving in there. Sounds howl from the glassless windows. Who is there? I scour the ground to see if I can find my Tata's childhood toys, scattered amongst the rubbish. *We often see projections of what our brain imagines we can see.* It can't be. My eyes begin to unravel what it is I am hearing and seeing. The patients are outside, they are howling, singing and clapping as they exercise around the gardens of the hospital. Behind the green gates, the ruins of Deir Yassin houses now make up the gardens of the psychiatric hospital on the grounds. The patients are walking into Yassini homes and inhabiting the spaces. They are touching the things that don't belong to them, the objects left behind. I am pressed against the gates, staring at this ghostly scene, wondering how anyone can recover in a hospital on the grounds of a place that has such a violent history.

I walk away from them, disturbed by the reality of what once was and yet, this is today. The ghost village I imagined is not the truth. The homes are still there, they are cordoned off and stolen by others as their refugees live barely five kilometres away.

We have the deeds to the land where the psychiatric hospital stands. We still have the deeds that show the land belongs to our family. They are sewn into the *thobe*. This is our land.

My unease makes me search for Hannah and Yousef. I spot them with Ibrahim and Mohammad. Fatima is with them. They are underneath a tree, and they have all stopped. They are starting to dig as the children watch. My mind flickers with images of buried infants. I run, hoping I am not too late. Fatima looks at me as I arrive, sweating. She encourages them to dig despite my protests. It is my fear, I know that. She has come too far not to see what is underneath, left by my Tata. What would a child bury all those years ago after witnessing such horror? I dread to think. Just as they are about to stop, they unearth pieces of decayed embroidered fabric, a child's doll and at last, a wooden box.

The brothers open the box. It is full of gold jewellery. On top of the rings and necklaces, there is a bracelet. It is made to fit the wrist of a young woman. Fatima reaches out her hand and takes it. She is crying and her eyes are fixated on the bracelet and then the sky. She is uttering words that barely leave her lips, but her lips are moving fast, as though whatever it is she is saying, she cannot say fast enough. I cannot make out what she is saying but I do not think she is talking to me. 'What shall we do with it? Should we put this back too?'

'It is Suad's so, it belongs to you, Layla, Hannah and Yousef. Why leave it back in the ground? She went through all this effort for it to be found and *alhamdulillah* we have found it.'

'I can't believe we found treasure!' Yousef says.

I take the box and close the lid. My Tata's treasure in my hands, discovered with my children, using a map she left on a dress a lifetime before.

I turn to Fatima to thank her. I pick up her hand in mine. She doesn't grip it with the vigour I expect. It is soft and cold. She has already left us behind.

Layla.
Chapter 10

'WE NAMED YOU LAYLA because Tata loved the name. It reminded her of someone from her childhood.'

Layla? Fatima's sister's nickname was Lulu. Her name was Layla. Tata called me Layla. My dad always told me she had named me, the moment he knew he was having a baby girl. Names are important. They recall the ones that have passed, the ones we love.

I realise that this was it. This was what my Tata had wanted. This is what my dad was trying to tell me. I had to return and not just stay in Jericho but return to discover the very roots of my Tata's childhood. She wanted the *thobe* to end up with Fatima. She hadn't forgotten Fatima's ardent wish to recover Layla's bracelet, so she embroidered the *thobe* as a map to find the buried belongings of the sister that her best friend lost that day. The more I thought about it, the more it seemed obvious. Palestinians have and continue to stitch dresses with family secrets and stories in, and it was a story Tata knew Fatima would see and instantly understand. And she did find it. These two women still understood each other only in a way they could. A treasure map after all this time! It is a map from my Tata to her childhood friend. She had never learned to read or write, so her stories would be passed down in *tatreez*. It made the most sense. It was a language only she and a select few others could ever decipher; only the Yassini girls could have found it and that is exactly what she would have wanted. I smile at her genius. I am proud of how she captured her life and how I inherited it. Layla. She named me after Fatima's sister. Even I was part of it. In some ways we lived for them and visited the places they couldn't. The timing was perfection. I found her and reunited them both. A wish they had both held onto for their entire lifetimes.

***

Fatima's burial was the next day, as is the way in Islam, for there to be a short time between passing away and the burial. I want to do something as Mohammad and Ibrahim have their hands full organising everything. Many families, friends and neighbours are expected to come. She knew so many people. The visitors, as is the Palestinian way, need feeding so I borrow Fatima's saucepans in the kitchen and work out how to use her gas stove. I am preparing before we go into the market. I already know what we will cook.

The children and I go to the markets, and I let Hannah and Yousef choose the cauliflower and aubergine from the stalls. We pick the shiny red tomatoes and small Palestinian cucumbers that look like they have been freshly picked from my uncle's farm. We choose lemons, mint and sumac for the dressing of the salad. It isn't complete without heading to collect the spices. We find the spice merchant; my children knew where to look as my uncle had taken them there before. We ask for the Al-Quds *maklouba* spice that both Fatima and my Tata had used throughout the years. We watch the merchant weigh it out and smell the familiar scent before it is sealed in the bags. We ask for two more to be made up so we can take them home.

We go back to her kitchen. We light the gas stove and gently simmer the chicken boiling in the stock. Hannah breaks the cauliflower off into smaller trees, ready to fry. Yousef is washing the rice grains in Fatima's sink. Together we place the cooked chicken, fried cauliflower and rice in the pan with the stock. Yousef smells the spices and adds them to the stock. The smell of *maklouba* drifts out of Fatima's window and fills the air with its familiar scent. We serve *maklouba* to all the family, friends and neighbours who pass through her doors.

The following days pass too quickly. We grieve for Fatima, and I miss her presence in our lives. It was short but profound and something I will never forget. A neighbour, that used to be and is now a part of my family, I was supposed to meet, who held the final pieces of what happened to our family that day and from then on since. We are connected in a way I couldn't have imagined. But it was selfish in a way to want her with us for longer. I believe that she has finally been reunited with those that she had spent an entire lifetime missing. Whenever I feel sad about missing her, this is what I remember to give me peace.

We are due to leave Palestine, but I don't want to go. I know now why he wanted to go home during his last few months on this earth. It was to be home. I could see now why he wasn't ever as happy anywhere else I had seen him in the world, and that was quite a few places. He had lived in a few different Gulf countries, in Jordan, Turkey, and the UK. After he graduated, he spent time in Geneva, Switzerland and Vancouver. He travelled the world, trying to find a home inside of it somewhere, but despite all the travels, here in Palestine was the place that suited him the most. In that moment I saw myself in him. Over the last few weeks, I had seen the same resemblance in his brother. My uncle was similar to him in his mannerisms and his voice. His days were structured around the prayers at his childhood mosque, where he would stay inside for at least an hour afterwards, sat with the Qur'an in his hands just as Dad did. Often, Yousef would join him and try to decipher the Arabic letters he was teaching him. Yousef had a talent for language in a way I never did. A language they continued learning together after starting with my dad.

I want the children here as much as possible. I want to teach them that they belong here, and they always will. I always used to worry that they would search for something, like I did once. I want them to know where to find it.

I am Palestinian and so are they. And so is anyone who has a Palestinian parent who has been exiled either in 1948 or before or after, even if they have not had a chance to visit. We are Palestinian and the greatest threat to our heritage is to lose that connection. I did not see it for many years, but as I get older and I understand the world more, this is as important as ever. I think of Yousef and Hannah. I wonder how they would find themselves if they believed they were only half as I once did. Half British, half Palestinian. That is their biggest weapon, to try and erode our identity. If your family were refugees from Palestine, you are Palestinian and you have a legal right to return. You have a right to return to connect with your culture and your heritage. I know this because it is a construct to make us believe that we should forget about the land. That it no longer belongs to us. But that will never be.

Throughout my time learning about *tatreez*, I have met other Palestinians scattered across the globe from Canada, America, Britain, and Europe. We feel the same and they are working with their own talents and in their own way to preserve their heritage. We may be scattered but we are united. Until there is a right to return, the Nakba is ongoing throughout Palestine. It is ongoing in my family, in the land stolen, in where we have left to live. In my Tata's illiteracy, in the water that is diverted, in the justice they don't have. In what was taken and never given back. In the millions of dollars stolen from livelihood and land and in the lives that we can never get back.

Before we leave, I find the children around the back of the house. They are planting orange and lemon seeds into the soil. They are replanting the orchard.

'This is what Sidu was teaching me, Mum.'

It finally sinks in. He wasn't teaching Yousef how to grow an orchard in the UK. He was teaching him how to replant it for when we returned home.

Layla.

Chapter 11

B ACK HOME, IT FEELS different. Everything feels different. It is as if it is no longer home. It is hard for those who belong to two different cultures to explain this feeling, and here I am, struggling. I know that I belong in the sense that I have lived here for almost all of my life. But I live detached from the place. I walk down the grey streets, listening to the sound of rain hitting the pavements. The swift changing of seasons leaves the skies laden with heavy clouds and a greyness that never seems to shift. Then the summer arrives, and the relentless heat of the sun warms up the old houses and the air is stifling. Whenever I close my eyes, I am back in Palestine. I am now physically far from those who have become the other half of me. It isn't just the people. It is the way of life. One structured around faith and prayers.

You can't understand why people stay in Palestine unless you understand the foundations of their strength. Palestine is not just a land. It is a land that is home to the ancient stories of the Holy Land. It is a place with its history and its future firmly planted in its religion. Not only is it about the preservation of land, but it is about the preservation of history and a future that people will live and die for. I think of Robert Fisk's interview with the Palestinian fighters in the 1970s. You have one of the world's superpowers fighting against you. We have Allah on our side. For me, my heritage is this link with the land and the land of our faith. The two cannot be separated. And as I reflect on this, I realise that this is the reason England does not feel like my home.

In the early hours before dawn I sometimes imagine I can hear the *athan* outside my window. I am now alone when I wake up before dawn or in the dead of night. Even the street lamps are turned off. This isn't a place where the worshippers walk to the dawn prayers. There are no mosques on the corners of the streets. The construction of the houses with their pitched roofs, hundred-year-old chimneys and Victorian-era alleyways are relics of a history that isn't mine. In the months following my return, I feel trapped under the roofs of these houses that smell of burning wood and cold, damp air. Living inside them, day after day, week after week, and something inside me feels like it's suffocating. I have felt this before. I left before but to the wrong destination.

Yousef runs down with a photo album. I had left the attic door unlocked and it stayed that way.

'Mum, I didn't know you rode an elephant?'

I look at the photograph. It was a time before the children were even thought of. A time they had never known of me, before. 'Yes, I did.'

'When was it?'

'Many years ago, when I was just a girl. I was looking for something then, but I was searching in the wrong places.'

'Where are you?'

'Thailand.' I look closer at the photograph. 'That was when I was in Ko Phangan. An island on the Gulf coast. I went there a long time ago.'

It was the other half of me before I felt complete. Before I realised I too was a Yassini girl.

Yousef and Hannah's dad has been working in the Gulf for some time now. I remember the last time I was there. 'Let's go and live there with the children.'

So, we prepare to leave.

I pack up the British house and clear out our belongings. I wonder how to feel when I donate the books and file the children's school drawings and childhood memories. We clear out the furniture. With every item leaving the place empty and behind, I feel free. It is our family here that I will miss. The friends our children have made. But there is a reason we make this decision. Even after all this time. This isn't home.

The plane lands. The air is warm and the city is lit with a thousand lights. We take the hour's drive to where our new home is. The landscape changes from skyscrapers to the early dawn mist of the shadow of the mountains on the horizon. The mosques at night are lit with green lights in their minarets, and then as day breaks their silhouettes are plentiful over the landscape. The landscape flattens out, camels graze in herds by the sides of the roads. Desert shrubs and patches of green appear over the sand after the last few days of winter rain. Wide highways cut through the desert, and we arrive at the place we are going to live.

I awake to the *athan* echoing through the skies. It isn't home, but it feels close.

Perhaps it is living in a country where most people do not belong here. They are scattered like us. They are scattered from wars and countries that are too difficult to live in, or they are not welcome in them through the ethnic cleansing of entire populations or places that are continually being erased from maps. And so, we gather here. The scattered hearts who have made it to a land that shares the echoes of one we cannot be a part of yet. A homeland that is being taken from under our feet. So, I gravitate to one that shares its similarities. In the sound of the *athan* in the air, in the balmy heat and date palms that line the streets. In the mosques and minarets that dominate the landscape. It is as close as I can get. There is a paradise, but you will not find it on earth. I know, I've looked.

The End.

Surely in the heart of every human being, there is a sense of scattering which cannot be brought back together except by turning to Allah. Ibn Al-Qayyim

Acknowledgements

Alhamdulillah for the opportunity to write this novel and for the journey that led to it.

I would like to dedicate this story to my Tata Nazher who this story began with; may Allah bless your soul – you are missed. I hope by sharing your story that we learn more about your life and the legacy you leave behind.

I would like to thank my Zaghari family first and foremost for generously opening their homes in Palestine and sharing their lives with not just me, but also a TV crew and a nation. Throughout it all, they are the ones who give me strength through their faith and unending generosity. They made it possible with a support that I will be forever grateful for.

Jazak Allahu khairan to my dad, Tata Zuzu and my uncle's Amu Hani and Aunty Maha and Amu Musa and Aunty Amena for being the connection between us all and facilitating this to happen. For my beautiful cousins, Jennah, Hiba and Lou-Lou. For Aunty Maha for sharing her personal story with us all.

Jazak Allahu khairan for Zuhdia and her sons for their generosity in sharing their lives with us. And for the welcome that we received; for making us feel that we aren't neighbours but family. Meeting you all was the light of the journey and now we are all connected. Alhamdulillah.

For my husband, who was by my side on this journey. May Allah reward you for coming with me to Palestine, every time, from the first to the latest time with a film crew! For being an extra hand on set, an extra security guard and being there so I wasn't on my own through this discovery. I wouldn't have gone without you.

Thank you to my mum who has been there always throughout every part of this journey of mine and I know at times that hasn't been easy... especially the backpacking part!

To David Vincent for selecting me to take part in the programme so that my family history could be researched and saved for many generations to come.

Thank you to Umar Al-Ghubari for his work on the Nakba and for being part of the research team that made both the discovery of my family history and the meeting for us and Zuhdia's family to take place. Your work is an essential part of our past, present and future.

A big thank you to Wafa Ghnaim for your dedication and passion to preserving the art of *tatreez*. Through your Evolution of Symbolism course, I learnt so much about *tatreez* and its importance in Palestinian culture. I also became a part of the *tatreez* community, which strengthened and connected me with the diaspora and for our shared love of Palestine and its people, wherever in the world we are.

For my editor, Siema, who is more than an editor; a sister and a friend who is dedicated and passionate from concept to publication and beyond. You are always there, and your support makes this all possible, so thank you. I couldn't do it without you... and I wouldn't want to!

To Jamil at Beacon Books for standing apart to publish the truth, where many others haven't. These works may never see the light if it wasn't for your courage and belief.

To Raees for helping us to create the final vision of what the books should look like. It isn't always easy but thank you for dedicating your time to find something that works for everyone.

For everyone who has supported me behind the scenes, and especially to Yousef Khanfar who has been a guiding voice throughout it all from the very first days of my writing about Palestine. I will never forget your advice on my first novel and every one since.

Jazak Allahu khairan all.

***

I finished writing this novel before October 7 2023 and the ongoing genocide in Gaza. It shows that history is not limited to the past. The Nakba, a brutal life under occupation and the subjugation of the Palestinian people has persisted for the past eight decades. I pray that the world sees Palestine, its history and people. This is the beginning of the end of a brutal occupation and the rightful return of Palestine to its people. For freedom of all those who are oppressed. For the souls we have lost, may you be accepted as martyrs in the highest ranks of paradise. May your stories live on as a reminder for us all.